Hey Diddle Diddle
The Zombie In The Middle

Janet McNulty

Hey Diddle Diddle The Zombie In The Middle

Copyright © 2018 Janet McNulty
Cover Illustration by Robert Henry

ISBN-10: 1-941488-85-4 (MMP Publishing)
ISBN-13: 978-1-941488-85-0

Library of Congress Control Number: 2017910566

Printed in the United States of America

For all the zombie lovers out there.

Hey Diddle Diddle
The Zombie In The Middle

Chapter 1

Ah. Peace and quiet. No mysteries. No ghosts. And no Jackie, at least until tonight when she returns from visiting her family. I looked forward to a nice quiet evening with Greg. We snuggled on the couch together, ready to watch some new zombie movie that had just come out on DVD in preparation for the season premiere of *The Walking Dead*, even though I felt that the show had lost some of what made it great in its first few seasons.

"Popcorn?" he asked.

"Sure." I took the bowl he had handed me and shoved a handful of popcorn into my mouth, dropping a few kernels in my lap.

"Ready?"

I nodded and placed my head on his shoulder as he hit the play button on the remote.

"Ah, this is nice," said a familiar voice. "And you two are so cute!"

We both turned our heads and found Rachel leaning on the couch behind us with a mischievous smile on her face.

"Oh, don't mind me," she said, waving her hand and motioning for us to continue with our movie.

"Um, Rachel," I said, "what are you doing here?"

"Watching a movie with you guys," she replied. "I thought that would be obvious."

"Rachel..."

"I'm bored," she said. "Now don't talk all through the movie." She walked around the couch, grabbed the popcorn, and sat between Greg and me.

"Uh, Rachel," I said. "We were trying to have a nice night together."

She nodded, looking at me with wide, innocent eyes. "Alone."

Rachel released an exasperated sigh. "I should have known this day would come. My Mel has grown up and no longer needs me." She wiped a fake tear from her eye.

"It's not..." I started to say, but she interrupted me.

"Now you listen here, sweet cakes, you're not going to get rid of me just like that. You need me, otherwise your life would just be too boring. You can't depend on him to always let you have a fun time." She gave Greg a bear hug and pinched his cheeks before giving him a playful smack. "You're just so cute!"

Greg and I shared a look. He took her unannounced

visits quite well, having gotten used to her comings and goings these past few years; and it's not like either of us had a say in when she would just show up.

"Oh, all right," said Rachel, "I can take a hint. Don't do anything I wouldn't do." She wagged a finger at me and vanished.

"So, where were we?" asked Greg in a teasing manner.

"About to watch this guy get torn apart by the walking dead," I replied.

Only two minutes had passed when we heard Rachel's voice from down the hall, yelling loud enough to wake everyone on the floor.

"Hey, Mel, your neighbor's dead!"

Greg turned off the television and I put the bowl of popcorn on the coffee table, kissing our quiet, zombie-filled evening away. We rushed out of the room and into the hallway, where I found Rachel standing in the doorway of my neighbor's apartment with the door itself wide open. Inside, we found a man lying on the floor, facedown, with his right arm sticking out to the side while his left was pinned underneath him. I knelt by the body, examining it, noticing a strange paleness to the skin. Not wanting to touch it, I took a tissue out of my pocket and rubbed the skin, wiping off what appeared to be some sort of white body paint. Using the same tissue, I turned the head a bit so that I could get a better look at the face, noting the same white body paint and brown smears from what I could only assume was dried blood, feeling trepidation and sorrow for my neighbor's untimely fate.

It wasn't him.

The hand twitched.

"Zombie!" screamed Rachel, startling Greg who only heard her and could not see her. She plowed into me, ripping me away from the body and we rolled across the floor, which must have been quite a sight for Greg who still could not see Rachel. Being a ghost, Rachel decided whether particular people can see her or not. Most times, she preferred to remain invisible while talking, stating that it is more fun that way. We crashed into a side table, rocking it some and knocking something off.

"Rachel," I scolded her, "what was that about?"

"It's a zombie," she replied. "Look at that dead look-ing skin."

"Well," said Greg, trying his best to talk in her direc-tion, "he is dead."

"He's the walking dead," Rachel said in a know-it-all tone. "Look at the dried blood around his mouth from where he had been chewing on live flesh—eating people alive!" She marched over to the body and lifted the head, pointing his face at me as though to prove her point.

Well, there went my appetite. "I'm sure it's just paint," I said. I joined her by the corpse and rubbed my tissue down the side of the man's face, scraping of some more body paint and held it up to her. "See?"

"Proves nothing," she replied, folding her arms.

"Is she still here?" Greg asked me, referring to Rachel.

When I first moved into the apartment building with Jackie, I learned that our apartment's previous tenant had been murdered when her spirit decided to show up. That tenant was none other than Rachel. Greg had helped us solve her murder and we had been dating ever since, having gotten engage last February. Over the last few years, he had gotten used to Rachel's comings and goings and accepted the fact that she was going to be a constant presence in our lives. He had also accepted the fact that because of Rachel other ghosts have a tendency to visit me, wanting their murders solved.

"Why is he asking that as though he can't see me?" asked Rachel, and I could tell by the look on Greg's face that she had not allowed him to hear her question.

"Because he can't" I replied.

"Oh." Rachel stepped away from the body and raised her arms. "Shake, shake, shake—here I am!" She made herself visible to the both of us and judging by the scream from the hallway that hurt my ears, she had made herself visible to everyone else as well. "Whoops," Rachel whispered, covering her mouth.

We all turned and watched as another of my neighbors ran away screaming, slamming the door to her apartment as she went in. Just great. The stories about this floor being haunted will continue.

I reached into my pocket for my phone and remembered that I had left it in my apartment. "Do you have your phone?" I asked Greg.

He patted his pockets and frowned. "Back at the apartment."

Not wanting to touch the phone in this place, amazed that my neighbor still had a landline, I headed for the door, but Greg stopped me. "I'll go call the police. Maybe you should keep an eye on Rachel."

Good point. I kissed him just before he left. With

nothing else to do, I decided to wander around the apartment, hoping to find anything that told me who this man was and why he was in my neighbor's apartment, but one question filled my mind: where is my neighbor?

Examining the position of the body in comparison to the door, I tried to retrace the victim's steps, while Rachel watched in amusement.

"I don't know why you're doing that," she said. "It's obvious he just walked in and dropped dead."

"Yes, but how did he get in?" I asked. I checked the door and it showed no signs of the lock being tampered with. "See?"—I pointed at the lock—"No tampering, which means that either the door was unlocked to begin with, or that this man had a key."

"I don't know him. Do you?"

"No," I said, studying the position of the body. A muddy footprint embedded in the carpet lead away from the door and to the general area of the body. Another footprint, not as dark as the previous, was two feet away at an odd angle. I found a third, just as strange and closer together. Following them and acting out how the man must have walked to produce such prints, I tried to picture him entering the apartment, staggering as he walked to the living area before collapsing. Staggering. Why would he be staggering?

"You found something!" beamed Rachel.

"Look at these prints."

Rachel frowned. "Zombies don't have a very good stride you know. They always walk like they're drunk."

"Exactly. And no, I don't think he's a zombie," I said

when Rachel's face lit up, "but his stride is uneven, which means he was either intoxicated, as you pointed out, or... something else."

I knelt by the body once again and noticed a shiny spot on the back of his head that I had mistaken for makeup at first, but what if it wasn't? Using the same tissue I had used earlier, I touch it against his matted hair and pulled it away. It's red, not a bright red from a fresh wound, but not brown either, meaning that he had this before he died and that he hasn't been dead long.

"What is it?" Rachel asked, ready to save me if the body twitched again.

"Blood." I showed her the tissue. "Someone hit him on the back of the head."

"Do you think your neighbor killed him and then ran off?"

I had no idea what to think. The man had not broken into the apartment, so either someone had let him in, or he had a key. I hoped for the latter, even though that would offer more questions, since I had never thought of my neighbor as someone capable of committing murder.

"They're on their way," Greg said, reentering the apartment. "In fact, they should be here—"

Sirens sounded outside the window in the parking lot just below us.

"—right now."

Rachel laughed at the timing.

Something caught my eye underneath another table that was just a few inches away from the man's hand. Reaching down with my tissue, I picked it up. It was a key. Before the police made it upstairs, I ran to the door and put the key in the lock. It fit.

"You need to hang onto that," said Rachel.

"I can't," I replied. "It should go to—"

Before I could finish my statement, Rachel snatched the key and disappeared.

Within moments, officers entered the apartment with a woman I had hoped to never see again: Detective Nicole Henderson. Where was Detective Shorts?

"What are you two doing in here?" she demanded of us. "You're contaminating a crime scene!"

"We discovered the body," I told her, not liking her tone.

"Is that so?" She stopped, took a closer look at me and frowned. "I remember you. You're that psychic friend of Detective Shorts."

"For the last time, I'm not a psychic," I said, tired of people calling me that. "And where is Detective Shorts?"

"Not here."

"I can see that," Greg chimed in. "He is usually the one who does show up, so, of course, we're concerned about his absence."

"Of course, you are," mocked Detective Henderson.

Okay. I know I did not make much of an impression on her when we had first met, but this treatment of us by her was ridiculous. "You know, you're being rather unprofessional and flat out rude," I scolded her.

"You tell her, Mel!" came Rachel's voice from the hallway.

Everyone turned around to see who had spoken, but all they found was an empty corridor accompanied by disembodied laughter.

The detective sighed. "Suffice it to say that he is on

vacation right now, not that it's any of your business, and I have been assigned this case. So, why don't you tell me how you discovered the victim."

"We were concerned about our neighbor and decided to check in on him," I began, knowing that I couldn't tell her that a ghost had discovered the body and informed me of it afterward. "We found the door unlocked and let ourselves in and that's when we found him."

"Is this how it happened?" the detective asked Greg.

"Yes, ma'am," Greg replied.

Her expression indicted her disbelief, but she kept it to herself. "Do you know who he is?"

Greg and I both shook our heads.

"And you have no idea why he is here?"

"No," Greg and I said at the same time.

"Have you seen your neighbor recently?"

"No," I replied, "which is why we decided to check in on him."

"How neighborly of you," muttered the detective and I guessed that no one was supposed to hear that comment by the way she said it. "When was the last time you saw your neighbor?"

"A week ago," said Greg.

"Any idea where he went?"

"No," Greg answered again.

"You two can go for now," said the detective.

"Well… did you notice how he is dressed, as though he had been to some sort of costume party?" I asked, not wanting to leave. "And his hair is matted with blood. It looks as though someone struck him in the head."

"You touched the body?"

I lowered my head at the irate tone in the detective's voice. "I used a tissue," I said, holding up the same tissue I had used. "I didn't leave any prints."

"You could have contaminated evidence!" Detective Henderson waved her hand at two of the officers in the room. "Get them out of here!"

"But—"

"If I have anymore questions that need answering, I'll contact you," the detective said to me as the officers shoved Greg and me out the door and barred the entrance, making sure that we couldn't reenter the apartment.

"That was very rude of her," Rachel said to me, when we entered Greg's apartment, slipping the key into my hand, and by the look on Greg's face, I knew he had heard her. "You should eavesdrop."

"We can't," I said.

"I'll do it!" Rachel said.

"I don't think…" I began.

"Actually, that's not a bad idea," said Greg.

"Listen to your fiancé," said Rachel. "Besides, what are they going to do? Kick out a ghost?"

Rachel vanished and I knew just where she had gone: my neighbor's apartment. Since there was nothing I could do, except wait for her to return, I picked up the bowl of popcorn and sat on the couch with Greg, resuming our movie, though I paid little attention to it as my mind lay elsewhere.

Chapter 2

I walked through the door to the Candle Shoppe—Mr. Stilton had already unlocked it, having opened that morning—and headed straight to the back room where the employee lockers were. My mind dwelled on the body Greg and I found in my neighbor's apartment, taking my attention away from my mechanical movements as I placed my jacket and purse in my locker.

"Mel!" Tammy ran up to me, enveloping me in a huge embrace, squeezing the air out of my lungs.

"What's that for?" I asked her, prying her off me.

"I heard about the body in your apartment!"

I hushed her, trying to get her to keep it down. I didn't want Mr. Stilton coming out of his office, demanding to know why we talked about a dead body, much less wanting to know what happened last night. "There was no body in my apartment."

"But the article said…"

"It was in my neighbor's apartment."

A confused look crossed Tammy's face and she glanced at her phone, which still had the news article on it, before relaxing and laughing at her mistake. "Oh, I got it wrong. Oopsy!"

The bell on the door dinged a few times as some people strolled in.

"So, what are you going to do about it?" asked Tammy, following me around like a lost puppy.

"Right now"—I snatched a box of tealights and shoved them into her hands—"I'm going to hand you these so that you can stock the shelves."

"But…"

I raised an eyebrow and Tammy stalked off with the box of tealights, disappointed at my lack of interest in the discovery of a corpse right next door to my apartment. It's not that I wasn't interested; I just didn't want her tagging along this time the way she did the last time I found myself involved in a mystery. I shuddered when memories of the sewer crept into my brain. The foul odor of the sewage still filled my nostrils. I shook it off.

After grabbing the inventory book (Mr. Stilton refused to change over to a tablet), I hurried out into the main area, stopping by the nearest shelf and counted the number of items on it, marking them down in the appropriate hand-drawn column on the book's pages. It would be nice if he would upgrade to the 21rst century. I meandered to another shelf, marking down the number of incense we have and what varieties. We will have to order more of the cinnamon spice ones.

I peeked at Tammy as she busied herself with stocking the tealight shelf, wondering what she was up to as she grabbed a candle, examined it, and placed it in a spot of her choosing. What was she up to? She shuffled tealight candles all over the shelf in a sporadic manner that seemed to have no logical reasoning behind their placement. Frowning, I walked over to her.

"What are you doing?" I asked.

"Making them look pretty!"

I studied the shelf and its rainbow display with all of the different colored candles spread throughout with no two colors sitting next to each other. Though creative, this was not what I had in mind when I had told her to stock the shelf. "Tammy, how are people supposed to find the particular scent they are looking for?"

"They'll have to hunt for it. It makes it more exciting."

A giggle sounded from the next aisle over.

Or frustrating. "I appreciate your efforts," I replied, trying to not hurt her feelings, "but perhaps we should keep them the way they were, that way it will be easier for people to find what they want."

"But that is so boring."

"Some people like boring," I said.

"I don't," came Rachel's voice.

"Fine," Tammy pouted, "but my back hurts from constantly bending over to get the candles out of the box."

An empty shelf was just below the one she was stocking.

I picked up the box and pushed it on the shelf to make it easier for Tammy. "There. That should help."

Tammy's face lit up and she hugged me for the second time that day. "You're the best!"

"Yeah, you're the best, Mel!" mocked Rachel, still laughing.

I walked away from Tammy to a more secluded section. "Rachel!" I hissed.

"Riiiiiight heeeere!" she sang, earning a few looks from two customers who could not figure out how or why the air sang to them.

I gave her a disapproving look.

"Fine," said Rachel, appearing next to me. "Stop a girl from having some fun."

"So…" I prodded her.

"So, what?"

"You stayed behind to eavesdrop on the detective."

"Oh! Right! They surmised that the guy had been dead anywhere form two to four hours, based on his liver temperature. They aren't sure about the way he was dressed. You know, that detective lady is no fun at all. I kept moving things around and all she did was blame the other living people in the room. Can you imagine. She wouldn't even give me the credit I was due. But I am happy to report that the zombie did not bite anyone."

What a relief, I though to myself, surprised that the voice in my head had a hint of sarcasm when thinking that statement. "Something tells me that she doesn't believe in ghosts."

"Detective Shorts does."

"You didn't give him much of a choice."

"Thank you." Rachel bowed low with her right arm stretched out to the side, mimicking an actor on stage as he accepts praise from an audience. "Though that Mordson woman still refuses to believe in me. I spent three months haunting her house and not once did she admit that she might have a ghost. She kept coming up with one logical explanation after another to explain my antics."

Rachel folded her arms and I'm certain that I heard her mutter a common insult for women who are stuck up or moody to describe the reporter who tried to ruin my reputation some time back. "But enough about me. Let's talk about you and your new pet."

"Pet?" I asked her, confused.

Rachel pointed at Tammy.

I stared at her. She has known Tammy for a while now. "She's not a pet," I said. "She is an adult."

"With the I.Q. of a ferret. No, wait. That's an insult to ferrets. I'm sure they have a higher I.Q. than her."

Thinking back on some of Tammy's exploits, Rachel did have a point.

The door opened and in walked Greg, spotting me and heading straight for me, the expression on his face stating that he had something important on his mind. "Hey," he said.

Rachel patted his shoulder, causing him to jump.

"Rachel's here," I whispered to him.

"He's a good boy," Rachel said to me. "I'll let you keep him."

Really? It was her who introduced us in the first place.

"Oh, you're so cute when your cheeks turn red," said Rachel, pinching them.

All Greg saw was thin air moving my head side to side.

"What's up?" I asked him, getting Rachel to stop pinching my cheeks and curious as to why Greg was here; he didn't normally visit me at work.

"I think I know why our dead friend was dressed the way he was," replied Greg, holding up a flyer.

I took it and read it.

Come Show Your Undead Side!

Zombie enthusiasts are invited to a night of fun and revelry meant just for the undead. Drink blood. Eat brains. And fill your desire for consuming living flesh while meeting others just like you.

When: Melgarden Park

When: October 15 at 8pm

Dress code: We're the undead. We don't have a dress code! But the best costume wins a $1,000 prize!

"Drink blood?" said Rachel.

"I don't think they literally mean blood. Probably something with food coloring," I whispered to her before turning to Greg. "That was last night."

"Exactly," replied Greg. "I found this hanging on a bulletin board when I got out of class this morning. Next to it was a similar flyer about an event tonight, a sort of Zombie Con."

"A Zombie Con?" asked Rachel with skepticism. "Are these people that desperate to get out?"

"Apparently," I whispered. "When is it?"

"Tonight."

"I'll pick you up." I kissed Greg.

"Aw, you two are so cute," teased Rachel, loud enough for us both to hear and giving us puppy dog eyes.

Greg smiled and left, since he had two more classes that day.

"Okay," said Rachel in an instructive manner, "we need to get you ready to take on the undead!" She stood in a wide-legged stance with her fists raised, demonstrating how to stab a zombie in the head, should the need ever arise.

I cleared my throat to get her to stop.

"What?" asked Rachel.

I pointed at a woman we both recognized, staring at me as though I had lost my mind, since I seemed to be talking to thin air: Jillian Mordson.

"She knows how to ruin everything," said Rachel.

"Talking to yourself?" asked Jillian.

"Does it matter?" said Rachel, but Jillian didn't hear her.

"Is there something I can do for you?" I asked. "Or are you here to gather more dirt so that you can write another scathing article of lies about me?"

"Oh, snap!" said Rachel, snapping her fingers.

"I'm actually here looking for some candles about this size." She demonstrated with her hands the shape and size of the candles she searched for and I knew right away what she wanted.

"Tealights?" I said.

"Yes."

"Over there." I pointed at Tammy as she apologized to the candles for having to put them on the shelves according to their scent instead of letting them be free to be themselves, to which Rachel busted up laughing and I shushed her.

"They're just candles!" said Rachel, but only I heard her.

Jillian leaned in. "You might want to be careful. Someone might think you've lost your mind."

"You're going to lose something in a minute, lady!" said Rachel, rolling up her sleeves as she marched toward Jillian, forcing me to hold her back.

Jillian smiled and I knew I had just given her what she wanted: more proof that I was nuts. She left and headed over to Tammy who now whispered to a purple candle.

"And she thinks you're crazy!" shouted Rachel. "Let me play keep away with her purse! It'd be hilarious!"

"Not really," I said, though the thought was tempting.

"Fine." Rachel crossed her arms and sighed.

Just then, a shriek sounded from across the room as Jillian slipped on a tealight that had fallen to the floor and landed on her butt, knocking Tammy off the step ladder, and as her arms flew, she pulled the box of tealights off the shelf I had put them on. I watched in horror as it fell, covering her head. Fuming, Jillian ripped the box off and chucked it aside, but she hadn't counted on Mr. Stilton running up to help her with his coffee still in his hand. The box snagged his feet and he tripped, falling on all fours while his mug flew through the air, spilling hot coffee all over Jillian's head before plopping on the floor next to her. People stared in silence, shocked and unsure of what to say or do as coffee dripped down the woman's irate face and onto her white, silk blouse, which must have cost around $500.

"Now that's funny!" shouted Rachel, laughing so loud that all eyes turned toward me.

Chapter 3

It's time. I grabbed my phone, shoving it in my back pocket after making certain that my ID and debit card were tucked away in the case. Taking one last look around, I swiped my keys and walked across the hall to Greg's door. He opened it before I had a chance to knock.

"Been waiting for you," he said.

"Peeking out the peephole, huh?"

"Maybe."

"We should go."

"Where's Rachel?"

That was a good question. I had no idea. After the accident at work, Jillian stormed out of the Candle Shoppe, threatening to sue us for damages or something, and Rachel disappeared at the same time. I had peeked out the door a few minutes later to find her on her phone calling a tow truck because someone had let the air out of all her tires. I'll give you three guesses as to whom had done it, but you probably only need one.

Before Mr. Stilton had a chance to chew Tammy out for causing the mishap, people congratulated him on the show, thinking that it had been done on purpose because who would actually allow someone to spill coffee on them? They almost pushed Tammy out of the way to get to the tealights and by the end of the hour, we had run out. Such a record number of sales restored Mr. Stilton's good mood.

"No idea," I said in answer to Greg's question about Rachel's whereabouts.

Greg closed his door and we walked to the stairs that led to the parking area, taking his car to the hotel where this Zombie Con was. It only took 20 minutes to get there. We ended up parking at the far end of the lot because every space was taken, which surprised me, since I had no idea there were this many zombie enthusiasts in this area.

We didn't have to ask about which room the Zombie Con was in when we strolled through the hotel's entrance. An employee stood by the doors, directing everyone to the banquet room, assuming that any who entered without suitcases had to have been there for one reason. Greg and I thanked her and we followed the crowd down a hallway and to a set of double doors. I stopped. No one was dressed like the walking dead, but various displays and booths were spaced throughout the area, each with their own unique decorations, adding their own flair to the convention.

I strolled by the first one which had a stack of books on it. Picking one up, I scanned the title, realizing that it was a novel about a zombie apocalypse, the first of six. The author stood behind the table, doing his best not to act too excited about the fact that someone had shown interest in his book. I smiled and placed it back on the stack, noting his disappointment, but I did not come here to purchase something. I didn't feel too badly for him because the people behind me bought two copies of his book after I had left.

Greg and I wandered around the room, scanning the tables, wondering where we should start, but neither of us had any idea how we would get any information here. I scanned the tables of zombie clothing (t-shirts, socks, hats, and sweatshirts); zombie food (don't get me started on that one); zombie bobbleheads (really?); and robot zombies because nothing says "I love you" more than handing your kid a self-moving monster hungry for brains. I spotted a booth with a huge crowd around it and directed Greg to it, curious as to why people huddled around it. I almost fainted when I saw one of the main cast members from *The Walking Dead* there signing autographs.

"Who's he?" asked Greg.

"The guy with the motorcycle," said a voice, a very familiar voice.

I turned but did not find any sign of Rachel. "Rachel, I know you're here," I whispered to thin air, garnering a strange glance from a woman standing in line.

Before I had a chance to steer Greg somewhere else, a

group of excited teenage girls came running up, screaming with glee, all holding a notepad and a pen, and
pushed me to the front of the line in their fervor, causing
me to crash into the actor. I said nothing. I didn't know
what to say. He just stared at me, wondering why I hadn't
handed him something to sign. Within moments, a pad
of paper and a pen shoved themselves into my hands
and a force grabbed wrists, forcing me to hold the items
out to him. He took them, signed the paper, and gave me
back the notepad; all the while I remained speechless.
Someone else handed the actor a magazine and as he
tried to sign it, an unseen force snatched the pen from
his hand—it wasn't his—and grabbed the notepad from
mine, shoving them into the hands of a very confused
teenage girl. She gleamed when she noticed the autograph, but before she could get too excited, the sheet
with the signature on it ripped itself off the pad and
found its way into my pocket.

I ran off and found Greg.

"What was that all about?" he asked.

"Rachel's here," I replied.

"Where?"

"No idea."

We ambled throughout the room, looking for any signs
of Rachel, but she remained invisible. Pausing in front of a
mannequin dressed like a zombie, Greg and I stretched our
necks, surveying the room, hoping to either find a glimpse
of Rachel, or learn where we should start our investigation
into the untimely demise of the dead man we had discovered yesterday. Arms wrapped themselves around me

and I panicked, whipping around to find the mannequin on top of me. I shoved it away, causing it to crash into a nearby table, which just happened to have a bunch of open cans of soda on it, knocking the beverages over and spilling the carbonated liquid all over the place. Laughter filled my ears.

"Rachel!" I hissed and the people at the table stared at me, perplexed.

"You should have seen your face!" Rachel appeared, but made it where only Greg and I saw her. "You were like…" She made an impression of my reaction and I swear I heard a snicker escape Greg's mouth.

"You almost gave me a heart attack," I told her, trying to get my heartbeat to slow down, after it had skipped several times from Rachel's prank.

"Only almost," replied Rachel.

Out of the corner of my eye, I spotted a couple, a man and a woman, handing out flyers. I pointed them out to Greg and when I turned toward Rachel again, she had vanished. Greg and I walked over to the couple and asked for one of their flyers. The woman gave me one. I read through the flyer, which remained vague about the details of the event and the location wasn't even mentioned.

"Why isn't the location given?" I asked.

The couple gave me odd looks. "You should already know," said the man.

"Why would we know?" asked Greg.

The woman snatched the flyer back.

I reached for it, but she refused to give it back. "I thought you wanted people to come to your event."

"How did you know where to find us?" demanded the man.

A strange feeling washed over me. As I looked around the room, I realized that we stood in a more secluded area, away from the main convention and very few people seemed to come over here. What was going on here?

"I saw you from over there," I said.

They both looked at where I pointed, not liking the fact that some stranger came up to them. "So, you weren't at the park yesterday?" asked the woman.

"No, why…" began Greg.

"We should go," the man said to the woman.

They clutched their flyers closer to themselves and hurried away.

"Wait!" I called out to them, but they had disappeared into the crowd and ducked out another door.

"You know," said Rachel, appearing behind us with a bag full or licorice dressed up to resemble a human brain, "this zombie food isn't bad."

"How are you…" I began.

"I'm remembering what licorice tastes like," said Rachel.

A man stopped next to us, gawking at the bag of licorice that seemed to float in midair on its own. I snatched it. He wandered away, but I knew that Greg and I needed to leave. We had learned nothing here and our only possible lead had run off.

"What's wrong?" asked Rachel.

"There was a couple here handing out flyers, but they didn't want us to have one. They mentioned the park and then ran away," I replied.

"What were they advertising?" asked Rachel.

"Not sure," I said and looked at Greg who shook his head, "but there was no location written on the flyer. I'm guessing that they were only handing them out to certain people, people who already knew where to go."

"What did they look like?" asked Rachel.

"Kind of like us." I pointed at Greg and myself. "And they went through that door."

Rachel vanished, leaving me holding a bag of licorice brains and standing next to Greg.

"Maybe we should go," I said to him.

He nodded and took the licorice from me, dumping it in a garbage can on the way out. I hoped Rachel found what she was looking for, since I didn't have a lot of information to give her.

Chapter 4

It was a little after midnight when Greg and I returned to my apartment, disappointed about our lack of new information. I had hoped that the convention would reveal something, but all I had learned was that, even within our community, we had a lot of people who loved zombie lore, merchandise, and other zombie enthusiasts.

"That was a bust," I said as I sat on the couch in a huff.

"Not completely," Greg replied. "We learned that at least two people did not want to talk to us."

"True, but what if they are not hiding anything?"

"Then, we'll try something else."

"Hiding what?" Jackie's voice spilled over the room and both Greg and I jumped, having not heard her open the door and walk inside. "Well don't all greet me at once," she said when neither of us moved to welcome her back home.

"When did you get in?" I asked.

"Just now," replied Jackie as though it should have been obvious. "So, hiding what?"

I knew there was no getting out of telling her. She did live in the building with me and at some point, she was bound to find out. "We discovered a dead body in our next door neighbor's apartment."

"Wait…what!" Jackie dropped the bag in her hand and it thumped on the carpet. "You said body. It's not him?"

"We don't know who it is," replied Greg.

"So where is our neighbor?" asked Jackie.

"No idea," I said.

She meandered through the room with her brows scrunched together, the way the get whenever she is deep in thought, trying to figure out a problem, but unsure of where to begin. "But he might know the guy," she said to herself, sitting in the big chair in the room, which still had some of my unfolded laundry draped over the back.

"He might have," I said, jumping up and running to my room. I remembered placing the key I had found in my neighbor's apartment in the drawer in my nightstand. I ripped open the drawer and the key was right where I had left it: tucked between a scrunchie and my phone's charger. I scooped it up, wondering why I hadn't tried this before, but now was a perfect time.

"What?" asked Greg.

I showed him the key and understanding dawned on his face as he remembered me stumbling upon it.

Before anyone could say anything, I hurried out the door and to my neighbor's apartment. Yellow crime scene tape had been draped across, forming an X and warning curious bystanders to keep their distance, but I ignored it, testing the knob. Locked. Of course, it was. I hadn't expected it to be otherwise. Taking the key, I slipped it into the lock and turned it, hearing a distinct click as the bolt slid to the side. I opened the door. Thrilled, I closed it, locking it again and went back into my apartment.

"It fits," I said to Jackie and Greg.

"So, they knew each other," Greg mused. "Now we just need to know why one is dead and where the other is."

Good question. I had no idea where to begin. I didn't even know that my neighbor had been gone, nor for how long. We weren't close and he tended to keep his distance from me after Tiny had helped himself to the man's food a few times, to which I had to put a stop to. "I guess we can call Jack," I said. "It would help if we knew the victim's identity."

Greg pulled out his phone and dialed Jack's number. After a few seconds, confusion crossed his face and he dialed the number again, with the same result. On the fourth attempt, he put his phone away, shaking his head. "Straight to voicemail."

"Does he have it turned off?" I asked.

"No," replied Greg, "I think he is just ignoring me. It rings for a bit before going to voicemail."

"Ouch!" said Jackie. "Hitting the ignore button. Now you know he wants nothing to do with you."

It seemed that Greg and I had used up our favors with Jack.

"I guess we can do this without him," said Greg.

Not quite. I knew someone who would help.

"What are you doing?" asked Jackie.

"Calling Tiny," I said. He picked up on the first ring like he usually does.

"Hey, Mel! Was just about to call you. Elise is throwing a Halloween party later and we wanted to know if you all would come."

"Um… sure," I said. "I need a favor."

"Another one?"

I cringed, knowing that I tended to ask Tiny for a lot of favors. "Well," I began, "last night Greg and I found a… dead body in my neighbor's apartment—"

"And you didn't call me?" asked in indignant Tiny.

"—and we need to know who he is, but Jack won't answer his phone." Yeah, okay, I probably should have called Tiny after the police had left.

"Won't answer his phone, huh?'

"No, and we need to know who the dead man was. He wasn't my neighbor."

"I'll get him," said Tiny. "You are coming to the party?"

"Wouldn't miss it," I said.

"Well?" Jackie prodded me after I hung up.

"Tiny will take care of Jack and we are all going to his Halloween party."

"Okay," said Jackie. "Now, perhaps you two could fill me in, in greater detail. What happened while I was gone?"

Smiling, Greg and I took turns telling her about the discovery of my missing neighbor and the mysterious man in his apartment. She listened to every detail and seemed disappointed—more like jealous—when we told her about visiting the zombie convention and how I inadvertently managed to get an autograph from one of the stars of *The Walking Dead*, all thanks to Rachel, of course.

I checked my watch. Two in the morning. "Guys," I said, stifling a yawn, "I think I'm going to go to bed. I to get up in the morning."

Greg walked me to my room and helped me into my pajamas and tucked me in bed.

We had already discussed the possibility of moving in together, but I still had a lease with Jackie, and refused to leave her stuck with the rent. Besides, my crazy Aunt Ethel had already threatened to move here if I chose to move into Greg's apartment. I couldn't leave Jackie alone with my aunt. There would be a homicide within 24 hours. Add to that the fact that Aunt Ethel had been talking about moving to the same town, leaving me scrambling to talk her out of it. One weekend a year with her is enough. Living in the same city as her would be torture.

Greg kissed me goodnight. "I'll make sure you wake up for work."

I glanced at my alarm clock, which had managed to set itself, and noticed a second alarm clock that had appeared out of thin air. "Something tells me that Rachel has already taken care of it."

He grinned and left, saying good night to Jackie as he let himself out.

Chapter 5

An annoying vibrating pulled me from my slumber. Thinking that it was just part of my dream, I rolled over and went back to sleep when it stopped. Just as I was about to drift off, the vibrating started again. Irritated, I looked at my nightstand and noticed that it was my phone making all the fuss. I grabbed it. It was Tiny.

"Hello?" I said, still half-asleep, and my raspy voice attested to the fact that I wanted nothing more than to go back to sleep.

"Hey, Mel, open your door."

I glanced at my clock. Five-thirty in the morning. I have had only three and a half hours of sleep and I have at least three more until I need to be up in order to get to work on time. "Do you know what time it is?"

"Time for you to open your door."

I sighed. The sun wasn't even up yet and Tiny wanted me to open the door? Knowing I would never be able to get him to leave, unless I did as he asked, and somewhat curious as to why he was here, I crawled out of bed and dragged my heels on the carpet as I walked to the door. "Okay." I mumbled and hung up.

Yawning once more, I opened the door to find Tiny standing there. "It is too early," I whined.

"I know," said Tiny, "but I brought you a present." He reached to the side and pulled Jack into view.

I stepped into the hallway and closed the door behind me, making certain that it did not shut all the way so that I wouldn't lock myself out. "What are you... you can't just kidnap people."

"He willingly got in the car," replied Tiny.

"Not like you gave—"

Tiny shook Jack, coercing him into silence.

There was no time for me to argue and I did need Jack's help. "Jack," I said, turning toward him, "I really do need your help. The man that Greg and I found—we have no idea who he is."

"It's not your job to solve every mystery," Jack protested, receiving a sharp glare from Tiny.

"True, but he was found in my neighbor's apartment and my neighbor hasn't been seen in several days."

Jack's demeanor softened. "Do you know when you last saw him?"

I shook my head.

"He was found in your neighbor's apartment?" Jack

asked, confirming, the tone of his voice telling me that his interest had been piqued. "Who is the detective on the case?"

"Henderson," I said.

Jack muttered a few uncomplimentary words about her. I guess he did not like her or had some sort of run in with her that ended badly. "Fine. I guess I'll help."

He folded his arms and the rustling piece of paper in his hands caught my attention. I thought back to the couple handing out the flyers and remembered seeing something similar in my neighbor's apartment.

"How would you like to snoop around in his apartment?" I asked Tiny.

"Glad to." Tiny stepped to the door and he raised his foot high into the air.

"Wait!" I said to him. "I have a key."

Disappointment filled his face and I almost felt sorry for him, but I didn't want the police to know that we had broken in there. I ran to my room and grabbed the key, hurrying back out into the hallway before Tiny changed his mind about not breaking down the door.

"I don't think this is a good idea," Jack said as I unlocked the door and ducked under the crime scene tape.

Tiny grabbed him by the collar and placed him by the doorway. "Stand watch," he growled and Jack nodded.

He stepped over the barrier with ease and followed me as I turned on a light and looked around the apartment, checking every table, counter, shelf, and nook. "What are you looking for?"

"Something I saw yesterday when I was here," I said,

receiving a frown from Tiny because I didn't invite him along. "A flyer about the undead."

"Undead?" Tiny stopped for a moment. "I know it's October and all, but…"

"I don't think it literally means the undead but is more of a Halloween thing."

Tiny gave me a disbelieving look.

"The man we found yesterday had been wearing makeup so that he would look like a zombie, but he wasn't really one. Maybe that flyer will explain where he had been before he died."

Tiny gave me a look. When it came to the world of the undead or walking dead, people became wary and didn't want to deal with, not that I blamed them. Zombies can't really be real. I just hoped I do not have to eat my words.

I took the east end of the room the man was found in and Tiny checked the desk in the corner. Bills, invoices, cut out magazine articles, bits of newspaper, manila folders, and a chain of paperclips stuck together were all I found. I picked up the bills, but there was nothing beneath them. Exasperated, I started to wonder if my memory was faulty when Tiny called me over.

"What's that?" he pointed beneath the couch.

I stepped over to it, noting the open *National Geographic* on the coffee table with the pages bent and crumpled from being read. It was dated 20 years ago. Getting down on all fours, I reached under the couch and pulled out a partial flyer; the top half had been torn off. It looked familiar, but I could not be certain if it was the same as the flyers that the strange couple had handed out last night.

"Is that it?" asked Tiny.

"I think so," I replied, scanning the words on the crumpled piece of paper. "See, there's an address there."

I had not way of knowing if this was connected to the murder victim at all, but even if it was not, it could be a clue as to my neighbor's whereabouts.

"You know"—Rachel appeared beside me, ignoring Tiny's startled reaction—"I followed those people around all night. It was exhausting! Anyway, I never was able to get a good look at the flyers you mentioned, nor was I able to get them to talk about what they were up to. Either they do not believe in ghosts, or they are very good at ignoring a haunting. I mean, I threw everything at them and all they did was find logical explanations! I'm sorry, Mel. I kind of let you down."

I showed Rachel the partial announcement I had found. She grabbed it. "Why didn't you tell me you found something?"

"You were busy talking."

"Wait. You're here."

"Yeah."

"Which means my alarms didn't wake you up," said Rachel.

"No, they didn't," I replied, wondering where she went with this.

"I have to go." Rachel vanished.

Jack coughed from the hallway and I heard a door close. Turning off the lights, Tiny and I ran out the door and I shut it, making certain that I locked it once again. We needn't have worried about being caught, since it was only Greg leaving for work.

"At it again without me," he teased, giving me a hug.

"Tiny stopped by with a gift." I pointed at Jack who looked as though he could freeze stone.

"He's showing me where he works," said Tiny, wrapping a beefy arm around Jack's slender frame.

"Yeah." choked Jack, wishing he could leave. "It's take your cousin's girlfriend's friend to work day."

Greg just nodded, deciding it was best not to interfere. "I have to go and may have to work late."

"See you later." I kissed him before he left, followed by Tiny and Jack, with Tiny keeping a hold on Jack.

I had no idea how Tiny was going to sneak into Jack's office at the police station, since it was against the rules for Jack to have company at work, but then Tiny didn't care about rules anyway.

I walked into my apartment and cringed when the howls of two blaring alarms attacked my ears. Realizing why Rachel had left all the sudden, I rushed to my room where I collided with Jackie as she charged out of hers in a panic. Dazed, we both shook our heads as we tried to figure out what had happened when the alarms jolted me back to the present and I crawled over to them, turning them off. I checked their settings. Rachel wanted to make sure I had gotten up, all right. She also had decided to play a bit of a practical joke. Both alarms were set for six in the morning, not eight, and had the volume turned to maximum. I'd kill her if she wasn't already dead.

"Why did you have to set them so early?" demanded Jackie.

I gaped at her. Normally the pinnacle of perfection whether in bedclothes or a fancy ensemble, Jackie looked a mess with her hair sticking out to the sides in a tangled heap as though a hurricane had gone through it alone. She swung her arms in frustration, showing off her shirt, which had bunched up around her midsection, while the legs of her pants sat at differing lengths. I had never seen her like this before.

Laughter spilled from the hallway but stopped the moment I turned in its direction.

"One word," I said to Jackie, "Rachel."

Chapter 6

I walked into work just in time to unlock the doors and let Tammy inside. She stood in from of the store, stamping her feet in the dusting of snow we had received during the night with her arms wrapped around herself in an attempt to keep her coat closed and ward off the cold. It was rare for it to be this cold in October, but it did happen from time to time.

"Sorry for being late," I apologized to her as I opened the door. Mr. Stilton would be in an hour later, which was why I had the key.

"It's okay." Tammy rushed inside, shaking herself in an effort to warm up. She took off her coat, and I noticed that the zipper had broken, which explained why she had been holding it closed.

I put my stuff away, glad to be away from Jackie's ire. She had spent two hours going on about Rachel's little practical joke and how it had prevented her from getting any sleep. Stifling a yawn, I felt her pain and reminded her how I, too, had only gotten a few hours of sleep. At least she didn't have to be at work today, which meant that she could spend the rest of the day catching up on a few Z's.

"What's wrong?" asked Tammy, surprising me with her concern. Most days, she proposed some hair-brained idea within moments of coming to work.

"Didn't get much sleep last night," I said, not wanting to go into much detail.

The bell on the door jingled and in walked a delivery-man with a gigantic box. I hurried out to the main room to greet him.

"I need you to sign for these," he said.

I took his electronic pad and signed for the box.

"I have three more," he said.

Great. Mr. Stilton's order had arrived. "Tammy!" I called.

She came out of the backroom.

"Can you help me carry some of these boxes to the back?"

She grabbed the first box just as the deliveryman returned with two more packages.

"Thank you," I said to him, but he just grunted as he left.

Once Tammy and I moved the boxes to the back, I looked around, wondering how we would reorganized the room to find space for the new stock. I remembered how Tammy had managed to organize the backroom during the summer. "Why don't you find a place to put all this stuff. You did a great job the last time."

Beaming, Tammy grabbed a box and opened it, pulling out a unique set of candles, and her lip pursed as she concentrated on the shelves, picturing how she would rearrange it.

Glad to have Tammy preoccupied, I went back out front in case anyone walked in. The first hour passed at an excruciating slow pace as no one walked in, so I pulled out the scrap of paper I had found in my neighbor's apartment and reread the address. I didn't recognize it. Pulling out my phone, I looked up the address on the internet and zoomed in on the map that popped up on the screen. It was an abandoned warehouse. Why would someone have an address to an abandoned warehouse?

I scanned the scrap of paper further, wondering if I could find more information. An address was nice, but shouldn't there be a time associated with it? Despite taking a picture of it and blowing it up on my phone, I didn't find anything else. It didn't matter. I needed to go there and check it out.

The bell on the door jingled. I shoved my phone into my pocket and looked up at the woman that had walked into the store. "Morning," I greeted.

She said nothing. She didn't even bother to smile and acknowledge my presence. Oh, well. Some people were like that.

I was about to pull my phone out again so that I could look up a satellite image of the abandoned warehouse when three more people walked in, followed by six more. We always get a few who stroll in, but we never get this many at once, except during certain times of the year;

Christmas being the busiest. Two more walked in. A minute later, a group of ten people strolled through the door.

What was going on?

I meandered to the door and glanced through the window. A sign hung outside with the words "Free pizza and a show. Purchase required."

Free pizza? We didn't have any…

I smelled something cheesy and delicious. Following my nose, and the people who had wandered inside, I discovered a table in the back with a stack of boxes, each with their own pizza. Without even having to ask the question, I knew who had brought them here, but wondered how she managed it.

Someone reached for a slice of cheese pizza only to have their hand slapped by an unseen force.

"What part of 'purchased required' did you not understand?" asked Rachel, remaining invisible.

The person stalked away, insulted. A woman, intrigued by the entire scene, approached the pizza and reached for a slice, receiving the same results. Instead of getting insulted, she laughed and tried again, chortling even more when Rachel smacked her hand again. "That's quite a trick," she said to me.

I just grinned.

"I'll take one of those centerpieces up there." The woman pointed at a high shelf that had a glass center piece with blue gemstones lining the bottom (made from dyed, tumbled stone) and dried starfish glued to the inside with a raised bed for a large candle.

I started to get the ladder but stopped when the

centerpiece floated from its place on the shelf and into the woman's hands, along with a piece of cheese pizza.

"How did you do that?" the woman asked me, the amused smile disappearing from her face.

"Um…" I began, trying to think of a legitimate answer, other than a ghost did it. "If I tell you, it will lose its effect."

The woman, and some of the others surrounding us, seemed to have bought my story.

I needed some help. "Tammy!" I called and she poked her head out of the backroom. "Come here," I waved her over. "I need you to monitor the pizza. Make sure that those who get some have made a purchase. One slice per person."

She stood by the table without protest, while I dragged Rachel away.

"What are you doing?" I whispered to her, hoping that no one paid attention to me.

"I saw how bored you were," replied Rachel, "so I decide to drum up some business."

"And where did you get the pizza?"

"The owner of the pizza place down the street was more than happy to let me have them."

I gave her a disbelieving look.

"Don't worry. I paid for them. I called in the order and picked them up myself, though he seemed a bit surprised. I might have forgotten to be visible at the time."

"Where did you get the money?"

"You know, when you have three rubber balls juggling themselves, you'd be surprised how many people throw money into the hat."

"Excuse me," a man pulled me away from Rachel, unconcerned that I seemed to be talking to thin air, or perhaps she had been visible at that moment; it's hard to say with her.

I allowed myself to be guided away from Rachel, and when I turned back, she had gone. "Yes," I said to the man.

"Can you tell me if these warmers are safe?" said the man. "My wife wants one, and her birthday is coming up, so, I thought I would buy one for her."

"They are safe. Is there something in particular that worries you about them?"

"Is there fire danger?"

"No," I answered. "Each warmer has an automatic shut off. After six hours it will turn off, regardless. I have one at home and accidentally left paper next to it and nothing ever started on fire."

He looked relieved.

"If you want, I'd recommend taking that smaller one and putting it on a shelf by itself. It shuts off after two hours."

He agreed and I grabbed the warmer I had pointed out to him and guided him to the check out. The check out! I had forgotten about it.

Running through the store, I stopped the moment I saw the line in front of the counter, but that isn't what caught my attention: items scanned themselves and bagged themselves while some unseen force took the payment. My mouth hung open. People within the line looked on with a mixture of amusement, trepidation, and curiosity. I mimed to Rachel, trying to get her attention and let her know that she was invisible. A few people gave me odd glances, forcing me to pretend that all was normal. I must have gotten her attention because she materialized in front of all the customers.

Some gasped in fear.

"It's just a trick of the light," I reassured them, but my voice didn't sound too convincing. It didn't matter. Before anyone could drop their items and leave, Rachel was on them, scanning their purchases and demanding payment.

A man walked behind me, heading for the door with an open pizza box in his hands, munching on a slice as he moved. Just as he reached the door, Rachel disappeared from behind the counter and grabbed the pizza box from the man's hands, while remaining invisible. "No! Bad customer!" she yelled, smacking him with the box while he just gawked at the empty air in front of him. "I said free with a purchase!" She shoved him out the door and all the customers saw was a man being pushed by thin air.

"Rachel!" I hissed just as Mr. Stilton walked in.

She stopped, looked around, and shoved the pizza box into my confused boss' hands, before leaving.

All eyes stared at me.

"I'm sorry, Mel," said a breathless Tammy as she ran up to me. "I tried to stop him from taking the pizza, but he was stronger than me." She ceased talking when she realized just how quiet the Candle Shoppe had become.

I cleared my throat. "Well, you were promised a show."

Tammy burst into applause, unphased by Rachel's actions, followed by some sparse claps throughout the store.

"It's all right, Tammy," I told her. "Go ring up the customers, please."

She hurried to the register.

"Mel," said Mr. Stilton in a growl. This was the second time something odd had happened in his store. "What is—"

"Now, you just wait a minute." Rachel appeared from nowhere and, judging by his reaction and the lack of interest from everyone else, I surmised that only Mr. Stilton and myself could see her. "It was my idea. If you fire her, you'll have a ghost haunting this place and your house for eternity."

Mr. Stilton's face went from anger to fear. "Just finish what you're doing," he said to me before running off to his office and locking himself inside.

I turned back to Rachel to say something, but she had disappeared again. At first, I was curious as to why my boss was so skittish around her and then I remembered that time Rachel had convinced him to not fire Tammy. I have no idea what she had done to him then, but he definitely remembered her.

The rest of the afternoon passed with a steady flow of customers coming in, looking around, and leaving with bundles under their arms. When the time arrived for us to lock up, I flopped by the door after bolting it, exhausted. Rachel's little stunt had worked, but she could have given me a warning.

A small piece of paper poked out of my pocket. The warehouse. I want to investigate it, but I have a class in an hour. Torn between what to do, I decided that the warehouse could wait, though I might want some company.

I called Greg. No answer. I dialed him again and received the same response. He must have his phone turned off.

I called Jackie next. "Jackie," I said when she answered, "how would you like to do some sleuthing tonight?"

"Sleuthing?"

"I found a torn piece of paper in the apartment next door with an address on it. I was hoping it could give us some answers."

"What's the address?" asked Jackie.

I read it to her.

"I'll meet you there."

"See you in a couple of hours." I hung up and forced myself to get up off the floor and grab my belongings so that I could drag myself off to class. I just hoped Rachel didn't decide to join me.

Chapter 7

I drove into the black parking lot of the abandoned warehouse, frowning when I noticed that the lights had all been turned off as well, leaving only my headlights. No other car could be found. Where was Jackie?

I texted her a message.

Be a few, came her response.

My phone chirped again—I had taken it off vibrate—this time telling me that I had a message from Jack. I opened it. *Name of victim is Malcom Bentley.* I thanked him and shoved my phone in my back pocket.

I looked out my windshield, not liking the entire situation and wondered if I had gotten the address wrong or went to the wrong place. Checking my phone's GPS and the scrap of paper that had the location on it, which I still possessed,

I knew I hadn't. But it was so dark. Why would anyone be meeting someone here? There was only one way to find the answer to that question, and that was to get out of the car.

I tried texting Greg once more, but still received no response. He must have been too busy at work to be able to answer his phone. Guess it is just us girls tonight.

I reached into my glove box for the flashlight I had always kept in there and had just gotten it out when...

"BOO!"

I jumped, banging my head on the ceiling of my car and dropping my flashlight. Cackling laughter met my ears, telling me just who had decided to show up.

"Rachel," I hissed, rubbing my head. "Did you have to do that?"

"Well, I didn't have to," she said, "but it wouldn't have been as much fun."

Right then, headlights appeared and Jackie's car pulled into the parking lot, parking next to mine.

"I'll be right back," said Rachel.

"Don't..." I tried to stop her, but Jackie's scream told me that it was too late.

Rachel was still laughing as I stepped out of the car and locked it.

"Don't you ever do that again!" yelled Jackie to thin air.

"I'm over here," teased Rachel.

Jackie turned in her direction, repeating, "Don't you ever do that again!"

"Are you ready?" I asked her.

Jackie nodded, though she still looked a little pale from Rachel's prank.

Turning on my flashlight, I shined it in front of us, using it to light our way as we strolled toward the warehouse itself. Silence loomed around us. There was no wind, no crickets, no sound whatsoever, just eerie silence, the kind that makes your hair stand on end, and the fact that it was almost Halloween did not help. Our light steps clopped on the pavement, while Rachel skipped behind us, humming a merry tune to herself.

I shone my flashlight on the building itself, noting the black windows, with a few that had shards of glass hanging in the frames, the remains of where someone had thrown a rock through it. Red, orange, and black graffiti decorated the faded lines on the exterior of the massive building, and judging by the brightness of the colors, I guessed that it had been done within the last week. A lone howl echoed around us and Jackie gripped my arm, hurting it. I faced Rachel.

"What?" she said, giving me an innocent, wide-eyed look.

"I don't understand," I said when we stopped in front of the entrance. "There doesn't seem to be anyone here."

"Did you read the address wrong?" asked Jackie.

"No," I replied. "I double checked it."

A nagging feeling that perhaps the partial flyer had been a red herring, or not connected to the victim at all, filled the pit of my stomach. I focused the beam of light on the glass doors but could not make out anything through the cardboard that had been taped to them on the inside. A loose-hanging chain caught my eye and I reached for it, holding it up for Jackie to see. Odd, that it would be here. I pulled it free from the door handle, wondering why it seemed to just be dangling there. Inspecting it closer, I noticed clean stripes in the grime that covered the chain, meaning that someone had handled it recently. I scanned the ground and found an open lock lying in a corner. I held it out to Jackie, showing it to her before dropping it back on the ground.

I tested the door. It opened. I looked at Jackie and she hesitated a moment. I stepped inside and she hurried after me, not wanting to be left alone in the gloomy parking lot. Paper, plastic, metal rods, nails, screws, and layers of silt coated the floor as we stepped through the debris with care, trying not to get a nail in our shoes. My flashlight found some footprints, fresh footprints. I pointed them out to Jackie. I could not tell how many people had come through here as there were too many and they spread out in several directions, making it difficult to discern where they went.

Jackie tripped over a rectangular piece of plastic and she skipped a couple of steps as she tried to get it untangled from around her foot. Stopping her, I grabbed the plastic and unwrapped it from around her shoe, throwing it aside as best I could. We continued. Dust floated in front of my flashlight, dancing in wavy patterns as we wandered through the first floor of the warehouse, past conveyor belts and machinery so covered in cobwebs that I wondered if they ever worked in the first place.

"It's kind of spooky in here," whispered Rachel.

"Says the spook," I said without thinking as I studied a discarded, and crumbling, box with a faded logo on it. I could just make out the blue lettering.

"Hey," said Rachel, placing her hands on her hips.

"You are a ghost," I replied. "You haunt places for fun."

"True," Rachel replied, "but we prefer the term 'living impaired'."

"Really?" I focused the light on her, not that it did much good, since she chose to remain transparent. "You're going to go all politically correct on me now?"

A clinking of metal on concrete rang through the still air, bouncing off the walls and sticking in our ears worse than syrup on your hands.

"What was that?" asked Jackie as we all three huddled together.

Good question, I thought and threw my flashlight's beam in the direction of the noise just in time to see a flicker of movement. "There!"

We crept to where the sound had emanated from, while I kept my light focused on it, but once we reached it, we saw nothing. I swung the flashlight around, lighting up the whole area as best I could, but still there was nothing to be found, except for a metal bar. I picked it up and focused my light on it, searching for some kind of clue.

"I don't understand," said Jackie. "Where did this come from?"

"No idea," I replied.

I meandered around the area in a circle, studying the inch-thick layer of dust and stopped. A footprint lay in middle of my flashlight beam. Kneeling down, I touched it, noting that it had been done within the last day as there seemed to be no new layer of dust trying to cover the print. Someone had been here. I moved my light in the direction the footprint faced and found another and a third leading to a staircase. I placed my foot on the bottom step, but Jackie seized my arm and jerked me away from it.

"What are you doing?" hissed Jackie.

"Seeing where this goes," I replied.

"You want to see where the dark and creepy stairwell goes?" Jackie's sarcastic tone did make me rethink my idea.

"Perhaps," I began, "Rachel wouldn't mind going first."

"I'm not going up there," said Rachel. "It's dark and scary."

A ghost who is afraid of the dark. That's a new one.

"Someone is here," I reminded them and pointed at the metal rod. "We'll stick together and not split up."

"Fine," said Jackie, picking up the metal rod and holding it up as though she were about to swing it, "but I'm taking this with me."

I led the way up the metal stairwell, doing my best not to make any noise, but the third step insisted on creaking a little when I put me weight on it. The steps seemed too clean: no dust, grime, or dirt. I ran my fingers along the cold metal rail, remarking at the lack of filth on it, considering this place was supposed to have been abandoned for some time. My flashlight flickered. Shoot! I hit it a few times to get it to stay on, praying that the batteries hadn't been about to run out. The beam of light strengthened.

Once at the top of the stairs, I focused my light on the second floor, finding overturned chairs, more scattered papers with faded ink on them, a wheel that looked like it belonged to a cart, and broken drawer from a desk. I moved further into the space, wondering just what I had expected to find. My flashlight flickered again.

"Not now," I whispered to it.

"What?" asked Jackie.

"Nothing," I said, smacking my flashlight to get it to stay on, pleased when the light came back. "Maybe we should check some of these rooms."

Jackie nodded.

I moved in the direction of what looked like an office but stopped when I got halfway there. The hairs on the back of my neck stood up and something told me that we were not alone. Grumbling caught my attention. Raising my flashlight, I pointed it as far as the beam would go, lighting up as much of the darkness as I could. I froze. Right in front of me was a line of snarling, growling, staggering—Zombies!

My flashlight died.

More growling rose behind us and we all turned around to find another group of the undead creeping towards us with their hands outstretched and their teeth snapping, ready for fresh meat.

"It's the zombie apocalypse!" screamed Rachel.

Jackie and I ran for the stairs with Rachel outpacing us.

"You're running from zombies?" I asked her, incredulous.

"Yeah," said Rachel. "They're zombies!"

"But you're already dead!" I yelled back.

Rachel stopped and vanished.

Before Jackie or I could reach the stairs, another group of carnivorous walkers stepped into view, blocking our path. I chucked my flashlight at one, striking him in the foot. I didn't bother to see if it phased him or not. Surrounded, neither of us knew what to do. Panic rose up within me as terrible images of my flesh being devoured by these things filled my mind.

Jackie hit my shoulder and pointed at an open door. We both bolted for it. One zombie reached out for us and I grabbed Jackie's bar, held it out in front of me, and rammed it under the zombie's chin, shoving him away from me before swiping the feet of another out from under her.

More came.

Geez! The movies and television shows were accurate. An undead horde is impossible to escape and they never stop coming for you.

I heard Jackie scream. One had her in its clutches. I grabbed Jackie's outstretched arms and yanked her free, dragging her behind me as I ran for the open doorway. Another zombie jumped for us. Out of nowhere, a shovel flew through the air, hitting the thing in the head, causing him to stumble and fall to the concrete floor.

"I got your back, Mel!" Rachel's voice echoed throughout the warehouse.

Jackie and I burst through the open door and into what must have been an office at one time. I closed the door, but the handle was missing and there was no way to latch it. I pulled out my phone and called Tiny, glad that he answered on the first ring.

"Mel, what—"

"Tiny! We're being attacked by zombies at the old warehouse! Need help now!"

The horde pushed against the door and I shoved my phone in my pocket, while Jackie and I pushed against the door with all the strength we could muster. The door gave way. We would never be able to hold it.

"That window!" shouted Jackie, pointing at the only window in the room. She took the metal rod from my hands, ran to the window, and smashed the glass.

I hesitated. If we let go of the door now, they will be inside. We had to chance it. Just as I sprinted from the door to the window, Rachel appeared, tackling the lead zombie from behind and placing the handle of the shovel beneath his chin. He whirled around, trying to get her off, but Rachel held on, and during the struggle, she took out a few more of the undead. To spectators, it looked as though the shovel had attacked on its own, but I could see Rachel's frustration as the zombie she had attacked refused to go down. She kicked the back of his knee and he dropped to the ground, allowing her to smack him over the head with the flat side of the shovel. I thought I heard a groan and watched as the zombie held his head in pain.

"And stay down!" yelled Rachel.

"Mel!"

I ran for Jackie, who had already crawled out the window and to an escape ladder. I stuck my foot out the window and placed it on the rung of the escape ladder but paused. Zombies don't groan. They don't act like they are in pain either. I studied the horde of undead more closely and noticed that they tried too hard to stagger as though they were unable to walk in a straight line. I grabbed my phone and turned on its flashlight, focusing the beam on the closest zombie, noting the beads of sweat on his forehead. Zombies don't sweat.

Risking everything, I ran for the closest one and punched him in the nose, causing him to stumble back, clutching his blooded face. Before I could do anything else, Rachel appeared with her shovel and jabbed another in the stomach before striking a third in the shoulder. Both cried out in pain.

"ENOUGH!" shouted Rachel in a voice so loud, louder than I had ever heard her use before, that everyone in the room froze. Pleased that she had accomplished her mission, Rachel shoved the shovel in my hands and disappeared.

"Jesus, lady," said the one Rachel had hit in the stomach, "do you have to hit us so hard?"

"Yeah," said another. "We're just having fun."

"Fun?" Rachel appeared by the side of the last one who had spoken, startling him so much that he hid behind one of his friends. "You nearly scared me to death!"

An ironic statement, coming from her.

Rachel vanished, once again.

"Hey, Mel!" shouted Jackie from the escape ladder. "What's going on up there?"

I poked my head out the window. "It's okay! They're not real zombies. Just reenactors."

"You've got to be kidding me!" yelled Jackie.

"What is all this?" I demanded.

Two people stepped forward, and despite their makeup, I recognized them from the convention the day before.

"This is a zombie walkabout," said the woman. "Every so often, Ian and I choose a place that is abandoned so that zombie enthusiasts, like us, can get together and pretend to be part of the undead."

"And so, you attack innocent people?" I asked.

"We thought you were newbies," replied the man, who the woman referred to as Ian. "Sometimes, new members are hazed a little bit before being allowed to join. Nothing too dangerous. We mostly just want to give them a bit of a scare, which is what they want anyway."

"We don't advertise it much because we tend to…" began the woman.

"Trespass?" said Jackie from the window, having climbed back inside. "And who are you?"

"Keri," replied the woman.

"I saw you yesterday at the convention," I said.

"Yes," replied Keri. "We had told our members that we would be there handing out the address for our next zombie walk. This is a charity event. The people here pay to be here and all proceeds are donated to a local charity. We have a local office." She handed me a business card. "How did you hear about us, anyway?"

I paused before answering, thinking of a reason that would sound plausible, without giving away my true intentions for being here. Remembering the text Jack had send me earlier, I formed my story. "Someone named Malcom Bentley told us about this place. Said that if we wanted a night with zombies, we'd find it here."

Neither Keri nor Ian reacted to my story, revealing anything about whether they knew the murdered man or not. For several seconds, I studied their faces, but they remained impassive, showing no emotion whatsoever, except for a split second when I thought that Keri blinked really fast a few times as though she tried to prevent herself from crying, but it could have just been that some makeup had gotten in her eyes.

The thundering roar of motorcycles reverberated around us. Tiny! I ran out of the office and to the stairs, shoving my way past others who had dressed up for the zombie walk and received a few glares in the process. Jackie was right behind me.

"Tiny!" I yelled once I got outside.

"Get behind us, Mel," replied Tiny. "We'll hold them back!" He raised a crossbow when some of the participants of the zombie walk stepped outside to see why a bunch of bikers had shown up.

"No! No! Stop!" I shouted at him. "They're not real zombies. They're just regular people who like to dress up as the undead."

Tiny paused but refused to lower his crossbow.

As I looked around, I noticed that his men held a plethora of machetes, knives, one even had a mace, lead pipes, and a nail gun. "Have you been preparing for the zombie apocalypse?"

"Maybe," said Tiny.

"You should do the same," Rachel said to me, remaining invisible. "You never know when you'll meet the undead."

"So, they're not real zombies?" asked Tiny with a hint of disappointment in his voice.

"I'm sorry I scared you," I said. "They're just..."

"Crazies!" said Jackie as she walked to her car. "I don't know about you, but I'm going home." She got in her car and left.

"Thanks for having my back," I said to Tiny, feeling bad that I forced him to come all the way out here for nothing.

I went to my car and tossed the shovel away once I realized that I still had it in my hands. Once in my car, I started it up and drove away having more questions than answers.

"Well," said Rachel from the passenger seat, "that was exciting."

Exciting wasn't how I would describe it.

Chapter 8

I squeaked into the classroom of my morning (that was one day a week) computer class. It was a requirement for graduation—the college required two of these classes—but I had been putting it off, since I am already familiar with computers and their basic function and didn't want to take a class teaching me how to perform tasks I already knew how to do. I also dreaded the two hours of complete boredom.

"Good morning, class," greeted the teacher as I sat at an available computer in the back. "Today we will be learning how to create eye-catching flyers in Microsoft Word."

Groans went up around the room. I glanced around at the people texting on their phones or taking selfies and knew that, like myself, they have been using Microsoft programs since they were five. I didn't understand why the university required such a class. Maybe it was a hold-over from a time when computers were new, but everyone has them now.

The singular sound of keys being tapped one by one caught my attention and I turned toward the sound, finding a woman old enough to be my grandma typing away at a speed of one key every five seconds. Okay, so, perhaps she will get some use out of this class. I just wished that the college allowed those of us familiar with computers to test out so that we didn't have to waste money on a class we didn't need.

I planted face in my hands as the teacher droned on about how to open a new file, showing every painstaking step, including how to choose your font type, font size, and font color. Someone shoot me now. Pull the fire alarm. Anything to get me out of here. I looked at the textbook for the class and realized that the flyer sample within the book was the exact flyer the teacher demonstrated on the projector his computer was hooked up to. How fortunate. Within five minutes, I had a duplicate copy of the flyer on my computer, and looking around at some of the other screens, many of the students had done the same. Nothing like an easy A.

I opened up my Facebook page and a chat box appeared on my computer screen. I clicked on it, wondering who would be sending me a message through the instant messenger.

How about a cure for your boredom?

Unnerved, I looked around to see who could have sent me that message, but all my other classmates were either busy texting on their phones or typing away on their own social media page.

Who is this? I replied.

Me. Duh!

Rachel? I looked around for her, but found no sign of her, which meant that she was probably sitting at a computer in the room, but remained invisible to everyone, including me.

Ding! Ding! Ding! You win the lottery!

When did you get a Facebook page?

Always had one.

I clicked on her name and was taken to her profile page, almost shrieking in disbelief. Rachel had her own social media page, set to public of course, and she has had it since 2012.

Name: Rachel

Occupation: I'm a ghost so I don't need one.

About Me: I was murdered, but don't want to go into that. My best bud, Mel, caught my murderer and now he is paying the price. There isn't much to do in the spirit world so I just pop in on my friend—did I mention her name was Mel?—and help her solve whatever mystery she has stumbled upon. Someone has to keep her out of trouble or get her into it. Ha. Ha.

Location: Wherever I am at any given moment.

What? You actually think a ghost owns a house? We haunt them. We don't own them.

I scrolled through her online page, surprised that she had over 6,000 followers, my mouth gaping open as picture after picture depicted many of our exploits, and some of them were of her hanging around in an area I didn't recognize. How did she get all of these pictures? I didn't remember her owning a camera, unless…

Are you the reason my phone goes missing sometimes? I typed in the chat box.

😂 *You really need to learn to pay attention.* 😂 😂 😂

I stopped when I saw her most recent post, which was a picture of both Jackie and me fighting off a group of people dressed as zombies, while Rachel stood, holding the camera, with her own scared mien. Jackie's frightened expression was priceless, but I couldn't stop staring at the mixture of fear and concentration on my own face as I swung the metal rod at them. It was a good action shot, and I wanted to kill Rachel for taking the photo while Jackie and I ran scared for our lives. The caption for it read, "Trying to solve the mystery of Mel's missing neighbor and the dead man in his apartment and we ran into—ZOMBIES! OMG!"

I scanned through some of the comments.

OOOO. Good shot! You should submit it to a photo contest.

Ha! Ha! You guys look so scared.

You always have the best pictures!

Yay zombies! Perfect for Halloween.

I don't know if your stories are true or not, but I love your page!

I typed her a message. *You took a picture of us! Really? My fans love this stuff! They don't even believe that I'm a real ghost. *snicker**

Great. A ghost who has fans.

This class needs to be livened up.

Oh no. *Rachel, whatever you are thinking of doing—Don't!*

Too late. Within seconds of her last message appearing, the image on the projection screen changed from the sample flyer the teacher had on his computer screen to a video which was a mix of music videos, funny cat videos, Hollywood celebrities' most embarrassing moments, and politicians shouting into cameras, all playing to the tune of *Yakety Sax* by Benny Hill. Laughter filled the room, and despite my best efforts, I couldn't stop myself from joining in. At times, the video sped up before reverting to slow motion, creating a hilarious montage of people jumping, screaming, dancing, and walking.

Unsettled, the teacher tried to stop the video and had managed to get the screen to go back to his tutorial, but Rachel was not about to be outdone. She jerked the keyboard away from him and the sound of tapping keys, that seemed to type on their own, echoed over the music. The teacher dove for the keyboard and grabbed onto it. I watched as he and Rachel had a tug of war over it that ended when she let go, sending him flying into the projection screen. Laughter roared through the room. The poor professor stood up, his shirt collar crooked, looked us all in the eye, saying, "Class dismissed."

Chairs scooted back in sequence and the printers came alive. I hurried over to one, snatching my assignment, and strolled past the desk, depositing my work on it along with the others within the class. As I reached the door, an image of a zombie running filled the projection screen and I paused to stare at it.

"Excuse me," said one of my classmates.

I moved into the hallway, apologizing.

Keri said that the zombie walk was a charitable event and that all proceeds were donated to some local organization. That means that she and her partner would need an accountant and an account to store the money. She also seemed a bit nervous when I mentioned the victim's name, though she hid it well. I needed to talk to her again.

Searching through my pockets—I wore the same jeans I had on the night before—I remembered I still had the business card she had handed me, and I pulled it out. I called the number.

"This is Keri."

"Keri, this is Mel. We met last night. You said that you hosted a lot of events during October. Was there going to be another soon? My friend and I were interested in signing up."

"There is one tonight, but it's a bit late for—"

"We'd be willing to donate a thousand dollars," I interrupted.

"You know, Ian and I could use some help at our booth. The event starts at seven tonight. Dressing up is encouraged."

"Great," I said. "I'll see you there." Perfect! I have a chance to meet with Keri and her partner again. Now I just need to talk Jackie into going and into letting me borrow $1,000. That should be easy—I hope.

Chapter 9

"I can't believe I let you talk me into this," said Jackie as we hurried through the parking lot and its dusting of snow to the entrance of the convention center, dressed in rags, torn jeans, and our faces painted to the point where we really did look as though we had rotting flesh falling from our bodies.

"You conned me into joining a beauty pageant last July," I replied.

"That was different. We were trying to solve a murder."

"And what do you think we are doing now?"

Jackie grumbled, mumbling something about pay-back being a bitch, but I knew she didn't mind dressing up like this. It was an excuse to get out of the apartment and do something fun.

We strolled through the double doors of the convention center, which had been dressed up to look like one was about to pass into the underworld with fake entrails hanging from the glass, complete with smeared blood and disembodied limbs. The doors creaked as we opened them and one of the fake intestines smacked me on the face, but I ignored as the amount of people standing in front of me dressed like the undead, just like Jackie and me, caught me off-guard. From wall to wall "zombies" meandered through the building, laughing, joking, and carrying on conversations about the day's events.

"Perhaps we should follow them," I suggested, pointing at a line of convention goers heading into a banquet room.

Jackie agreed and we fell in line with a group of people who were either dressed like zombies or sported a pair of worn out jeans and tattered shirts, carrying fake axes and machetes. It seemed that some preferred to dress up as zombie hunters, while most wanted to pretend to be an animated corpse.

A snarling noise sounded in my ear and I jumped, forgetting that I was surrounded by zombie enthusiasts as I was reminded of the night before and the scare that I had received thinking that the apocalypse had come into fruition.

"Sorry," apologized the man behind me, while holding onto his girlfriend. "Didn't mean to scare you."

"No worries," I replied.

"Is this your first time here?"

"Yes," I said. "We heard about this event and thought that we would come out for a night of fun."

"No better way to do it," replied the girlfriend.

A thought entered my mind. "This is quite an event for first time organizers."

"First time?" said the man. "Keri and Ian have been organizing events like these for a few years now. They do try to keep it where only those who are zombie enthusiasts like us know about them, but we are always looking for new participants."

"Oh," I said, "I'm sorry. I don't know why I thought that they had never organized an event like this before."

"That's because you're probably thinking of Malcolm," said the girlfriend.

"Malcolm?" I asked, elated that they knew the murder victim.

"Yeah," continued the girlfriend, "he used to be the one that organized all this with Keri. Ian always stayed in the background. I heard he went missing."

"He was murdered," said Jackie.

"Murdered?" both the man and his girlfriend said at the same time, shocked.

"Yeah," I said, "there was an article in the paper."

"That's terrible," said the couple.

"I'm sorry," I said. "I didn't mean to upset you."

"No, not at all," said the girlfriend. "Malcolm was a true zombie enthusiast. He loved these sorts of get togethers and always made sure that newbies, like you, were welcome. And it wasn't just about letting people like us gather and have some fun, but also about the charities as well."

"Charities?" said Jackie.

"Yeah," replied the man. "He always made sure that all proceeds went to the United Children's Cancer Research Fund. He was a very generous guy."

"So, you knew him?" I asked.

"Not well," replied the man, "but we met him at a few of these events."

"Poor Keri," said the man's girlfriend. "She's handling this really well."

More people pushed past us as the room filled up.

"We better get in there," said the man. "Enjoy your evening."

I watched as they disappeared into the crowd, mingling with the other participants who were dressed up as their favorite ambling dead person or zombie hunter. Jackie and I followed suit and found a place to stand back and watch. Once in the main room, I couldn't believe some of the creative thing people had created to sell—all proceeds went to the chosen charitable organization of course—and found myself mesmerized by the brain cakes, complete with streaks of red icing the mimicked blood; disembodied feet quesadillas, and who had the time to cut tortillas into the shape of feet is beyond me; intestines, which was nothing more than bratwurst dressed up to look like your insides; and people hash, and I really hoped that the meat was just hamburger dressed up like the remains of a human being. While I gawked at the dietary offerings, Jackie perused the amount of books about zombie survival, t-shirts, bookbags, flipflops with half-eaten heads on them, makeup, costumes, posters, journals, pens, pads of paper, glassware, and independently produced movies. They had some creative stuff here and I had to give them props for it and all the work that went into organizing them.

People shouting drew my attention and I jerked Jackie's

focus to the stage in the room where a play seemed to be taking place. Two people dressed in ratty clothes, pretending to be survivors, struggled to escape from five of the undead that lolled toward them, salivating for brains. It was hokey and kind of dumb, but interesting as well. Many within the room watched with mild bemusement.

"Oh, my gosh!" Rachel appeared beside me and grabbed my arm. "You have to come with me."

"Bu—"

I never got the chance to protest or argue with her as she dragged me through the crowd of people dressed as animated corpses, many of whom gave me reprimanding stares, telling me that they did not see Rachel. Where was she taking me? I soon had an answer to my question when I found myself thrust into the cast of *iZombie*. How did Keri and Ian manage this?

I apologized for almost knocking over the actress who played the main character, Liv More; she looked so different without all that makeup on.

"This is my friend, Mel," said Rachel, introducing us, and judging by the confused looks around me, I knew that none of them saw her, "and she is going to be a great film director someday. So, you all take note. Oh! I almost forgot."

Rachel grabbed a pen and notepad from a nearby table and thrust into each of the cast's hands, demanding an autograph. They each took the pen, looking around confused and wondering how these items moved themselves, while giving me questioning glances. I just shrugged my shoulders. What else could I do? Rachel was a ghost with a mission. When she reached the last person, he paused, unsure if he should trust the floating pen and pad of paper.

"It's not going to sign itself," said Rachel, shaking the pen at him.

He took it and signed his autograph.

"I have to say," said the main actress in an uneasy voice to me, "that your ability to throw your voice is amazing."

"Throw your voice?" Rachel replied. "This isn't some ventriloquist act! What is she talking about?" Rachel glared at me.

"They can't see you," I told her out of the side of my mouth.

"Oh." She made herself visible, garnering several gasps from the cast and those surrounding us. "What does a ghost have to do to get some attention around here?"

"Pretty much what you are already doing," I whispered to her.

She scoffed at me, but something caught her attention and she shrieked with excitement before disappearing, with the autographs, of course, leaving me to bear the brunt of people's confused state and questions.

"The special effects around here are unreal," I said, hurrying away, desperate to get away from the frenzy and accusatory stares.

I found Jackie stuck between two men who seemed to be hitting on her, and she looked uncomfortable as though she wanted to run away. "Sorry about that," I apologized to her once I reached her.

"Excuse me," said one of the men to me, "we were talking to her."

"And you can leave," I told him.

Irritated, he and his friend stalked away, annoyed by my interrupting their plans.

"What was that all about?" Jackie asked me.

"Rachel being Rachel."

Jackie nodded her head as though that explained everything, and it usually did.

I spotted Keri sitting at a booth with a cashbox. That must be where you could go to make a final donation, and I had promised her that I was interested in helping her with her cause. Nudging Jackie, I urged her to follow me and she grimaced, knowing that it meant pulling out her checkbook, or debit card in this case. "I'll pay you back," I reminded her.

She grunted.

After several minutes or pushing, shoving, and forcing our way through the packed room, we managed to reach the booth where Keri greeted us with a white smile, showcasing her perfectly straight and snowy teeth.

"Hey," I greeted her, trying to sound as cheerful as she did, while Jackie remained silent.

"I love the costumes," said Keri.

"Thank you," I replied and pointed at Jackie. "She is the makeup artist."

"Well, we are pleased to have you contribute to the Children Cancer Fund."

Jackie pulled out her card, frowning at Keri's not so subtle reminder about my promised $1000 donation. "Do you take credit cards?"

"Of course." Keri pulled out her phone with one of

those credit card readers attached to it. Within seconds, she had taken the payment, having Jackie sign for the transaction on her phone, and texted her a receipt. "For tax purposes," she reminded us.

Jackie smiled. At least that was one deduction she could claim next spring when filing.

"Anyway," Keri continued as though we had been having a conversation earlier, "as you can see, this is a place for people like us to let loose and unwind and make friends. Some come to share their wares or talents, but to have a booth here, they have to agree to send ten percent of the proceeds to our chosen charity, instead of paying a fee to be here. It's all for a good cause, as you well-know."

"I noticed the cast from a known television show here," I said.

Keri smiled. "Sometimes, I am able to get a few celebrities to show up. It really helps with promotion."

"You know," I decided to risk bringing up Malcolm to see what her reaction would be and it was the reason for Jackie and me being here, "we met this charming couple—real zombie enthusiasts—and they mentioned that someone called Malcolm wasn't here. Is he a…"

Keri's expression changed, morphing from one of curiosity to sadness and trepidation.

"You know him," said Jackie, and it wasn't a question.

"Malcolm is a partner of ours. He usually sets all this up, but he disappeared a few days ago and hasn't been answering his cell; so, Ian and I had to take over tonight's event. I didn't want to cancel it."

"He was murdered!" Rachel's voice echoed around us

and I gave her a disapproving glare. She just shrugged her shoulders and responded me an innocent look.

"What?" Keri said, surprised.

"I'm sorry," I said. "I don't like being the bearer of bad news, but earlier this week, I found a man murdered in my neighbor's apartment and the police identified him as Malcom Bentley. It never occurred to me that he could be known to you until just now. Is he the same…"

"Yes," Keri replied in a small voice.

"I know this is hard, but do you know why he was in my neighbor's apartment?" I asked.

"Why?" replied Keri.

"He had a key to the place, but as far as I know, my neighbor didn't have any family or friends living here who would have access to his home."

"I don't know." Keri looked around and she seemed nervous. I didn't want her clamming up, so I remained silent, hoping she would continue and was thankful when she did. She pulled Jackie and me to the side, not wanting any prying ears to overhear us. "I don't know about your neighbor, but Malcolm had been acting strange lately."

"Strange?" asked Jackie.

"Jumpy. Like he was afraid someone was after him. I asked him about it one day, but he refused to talk to me. All I know is he said he had a friend in town that he was going to stay with."

Maybe my neighbor did have a friend he trusted enough to give a key to his apartment to.

"He never said what bothered him?" I asked.

Keri shook her head. "Malcolm tended to keep to

himself. He wouldn't tell me what was wrong, but there was that incident last week."

"Incident?"

"Yeah, some guys showed up wanting to talk to him. They never gave their names, but one had a beard and wore this faded red, leather jacket. They just said that they needed to talk to Malcolm about some financial matters. I didn't think much of it at the time, but when I told Malcolm, he seemed upset and furious. Later that day, I overheard him on his phone saying that he didn't owe anyone anything."

"And you have no idea what he meant by that?"

Keri shook her head.

"Why didn't you mention him last night?" I asked.

"Ian…"

"Keri?" Ian walked up to us, perplexed as to why his partner wasn't near the donations booth. "What's going on?"

Unable to hold it in any longer, Keri broke down in tears and I knew that our cue to leave had arrived, so I nodded at Jackie, but before either of us could walk away, we found ourselves face to face with Detective Henderson. Great.

"She says that Malcolm is dead," Keri wailed into Ian's shoulder and he embraced her in a comforting hug, but something about it seemed odd.

"Miss Summers," Detective Henderson said to me in an irritated tone, "what are you doing here?"

"Having a night of fun," I said, evading her obvious question and the one I knew she would ask next.

She scowled at me but let me off the hook only because she had more pressing matters to attend. "You two," she said to Keri and Ian, "I need you to come with me to answer a few questions."

"What is this about?" asked Ian.

"Your business partner, Malcolm Bentley, was found murdered two days ago. I can get a warrant, but I would prefer to not go that route."

Ian kept a protective arm around the emotional Keri and steered her out of the convention area, accompanied by a couple of officers.

"Miss Summers," Detective Henderson turned toward me, "enjoy your evening."

Her curt tone served as a warning for me to stay out of it, as though that was ever going to happen.

"I don't trust him," Rachel said, materializing beside me with her arms crossed.

"Who?" I asked her.

"Him!" She pointed at Ian.

"He seems to be cooperating," I told her.

"Please," scoffed Rachel. "She"—she pointed at Keri—"is obviously upset by the news you gave her, but he never batted an eye at learning that his friend is dead."

Rachel had a point, but there was one problem. "We have no proof of anything. Maybe he's one of those who never shows emotions in public."

Rachel rolled her eyes and vanished, startling a group of girls who happened to be strolling by.

My stomach growled and I glanced around at my choices for food, losing my appetite with each passing second. "Why don't you and I," I said to Jackie, "get some real food."

"Best idea all night," replied Jackie. "This makeup is starting to itch."

I couldn't agree more.

Chapter 10

I turned the water off in the shower and grabbed my towel, drying myself and doing my best to wring the water out of my long hair. My phone chirped at me and I picked it up. A message appeared from Jack. Figuring it must be important, I opened it.

Did some checking, found that the victim had some financial trouble. Over $100,000 worth.

Over $100,000? Who did he owe it to?

You think you can tell Tiny to leave me alone?

I chuckled at that last message. I decided that I would let him deal with Tiny's company a little bit longer. After wrapping my towel around me, I went to my room and got dressed, throwing my hair up into a messy bun and looking forward to crawling into bed as I yawned. My phone rang. I didn't recognize the number but answered it anyway. "Hello?" I said.

"Mel?"

The voice sounded somewhat familiar and the sorrowful tone was unmistakable.

"Yes?" I said.

"It's Keri."

My exhaustion disappeared as though it had never existed. "What can I do for you?" I asked.

"Can we meet somewhere?"

"Sure. Name the place nd I'll be there."

"The truck stop just outside of town."

"I'll be there in an hour."

She hung up. Wasting no time, I grabbed my phone and keys and left my room, taking a quick glance at Jackie's door, but it was closed, meaning that she had gone to bed. I didn't want to wake her. For a moment, I considered asking Greg to come with me, but knew he would be in bed by now if he were home and I didn't want to wake him either. It was just a simple meeting. I left my apartment and hurried down to the parking area where my car was.

The truck stop was a 24-hour place just ten miles outside the city's edge. It wasn't far and the interstate gets you there within 20 minutes. I pulled in, passing the lines of parked trucks and found a space not too far from the restaurant entrance. I found Keri sitting on a bar stool at the counter the moment I walked through the door.

"Iced tea," I said to the waitress when she looked at

me, and she frowned, disappointed that I hadn't ordered anything more, and probably thinking she was going to get a lousy tip because of it. Truth was, I just wasn't hungry.

"Is everything okay?" I asked Keri.

She shook her head, and judging by the tear-stained face, I knew she had been crying.

"Tell me what happened." Learning about the death of her friend would not have been enough to force her to call me out here in the middle of the night.

"Some guys showed up at my office tonight," she said.

"Some guys? Did you know them?"

"No!"

A few heads turned our way at her outburst and she silenced herself, embarrassed about attracting so much attention. The waitress gave me an odd look as she placed a glass of iced tea in front of me, and I handed her a couple of dollar bills to pay for it. Yep, she suspected she wouldn't get much of a tip, or so her scowl indicated.

"Why don't you start from the beginning," I said.

Keri took a deep breath and exhaled, releasing a deep sigh. "After I learned of Malcolm's death, I just wanted to be alone, so I went back to my office. It's a small building where we set up shop so that people could contact us about fundraisers, and so we could look more offivcial. I heard a commotion in Malcolm's office and couldn't think of why anyone would be in there, so I checked it out. These guys were searching the place."

"Did they trash it?"

"No," Keri said. "but they looked through drawers and stuff. They were looking for something. One of them noticed me and demanded to know where Malcolm was. I asked them why and all they said was that he was a friend of theirs."

"And you didn't believe them."

"Of course not! Malcolm never hung out with people like that and something about them didn't seem right."

"Did they say who they were?"

"No, I have no names. They just said that he owed them some money. I told them that was ridiculous and that it would be difficult to get it all back, since Malcolm is dead."

"Bet they weren't happy about that."

"They accused me of lying, but I handed them that detective's card and told them they could talk to her if they wanted proof. They tossed it aside, saying that it is now my problem."

"So, they expect you to pay?" I asked.

"I don't know, but I don't understand how Malcolm could owe money to anyone. He wasn't the type to just spend it. He hung onto almost every penny he made."

"Now, you said that your zombie walks are done for charity," I said, voicing a curiosity of mine, "so I'm assuming you all have other jobs?"

"Yes," said Keri. "Most days, I work as a temp at some office. I've had difficulty finding permanent work, but a lot of offices need temps for when someone goes on vacation or they end up with a vacancy that hasn't been filled. Malcolm worked as a night security guard. Said it was the easiest job he ever had. All he did was sit behind a desk at one of those expensive apartment buildings and watch security cameras and hitting the buzzer to let people who lived there inside. Sometimes, he'd watch internet videos on his phone."

"And Ian," I asked.

"Works somewhere. He said he got a new job but won't tell me where."

"So, how do you keep your charity running?"

"Legally, we're not a charity. We just raise funds that we donate to a charity. About twenty-five percent of all proceeds are reinvested and used to pay for the small offices we rent and to set up another event. We have to rent the places we host our zombiefest events and then there is the advertising. Five percent is doled out and paid to each of us. It isn't much. More of a small stipend for our time spent there, but we all do it more out of a desire to help others. Malcolm usually just donated his share. Which is why I cannot believe that he would owe money to anyone."

"So, there is no chance that he ever gambled or maybe has a loved one who needed a hospital stay?"

"Gambling? No way. As for a loved one… I don't know. He never talked about his past much."

"How is Ian taking all of this?"

Keri blew her nose and dried a few more tears before answering. "I don't know. He didn't say much, and after the detective left, he left, saying that he had to clear his head."

Understandable. Finding out that someone you know and worked with was not only dead, but murdered, was not something you just got over. He probably had to think things through or didn't want to break down in front of Keri, who was in tears and emotionally distraught.

"It's going to be okay," I told her, but my words felt empty. It's one of those things you say when you want to comfort someone, but you know that there is no way you can take away their pain. "I know someone who might be able to look into these men and maybe they were just lying. Is there anything else you can tell me about Malcolm that may solve this mystery?"

Keri shook her head. "He was just agitated when I last saw him, kept saying something about 'double aces'. Wouldn't tell me why, but I could tell that he was very upset." She stood up, doing her best not to cry again. "I'm sorry. It's late and I have to work in the morning."

"Drive carefully," I told her, concerned about her ability to drive with her emotions running so high.

"Don't worry about me."

I watched Keri leave and looked at my watch. Almost three in the morning. There goes another night's sleep. Knowing I needed to get home myself, I got up and dropped a couple of bucks in the tip jar before leaving. It wobbled. Turning around, I stared at it a minute before heading for the door. The tip jar followed me, sliding across the counter of its own accord. Stopping, I glanced around, but saw no sign of Rachel or any evidence of it being rigged to move across the counter. I took another step and the tip jar inched closer in tune to my movements.

"Rachel!" I hissed, hoping no one heard or watched me.

"There's a ten hidden in your phone's case," came her voice, but she remained invisible.

Perturbed, but knowing I would never get out of it, I

pulled off my phone's case and stuck the ten-dollar bill I had hidden in there in the tip jar. "You have got to quit going through my things," I whispered.

"But it's so much fun," said Rachel.

"And you still owe me for the money you took from my wallet earlier this year."

"Details."

I left the truck stop and got in my car when I thought of something. Hoping Rachel was still nearby and would hear me, I asked, "Will you make sure Keri gets home safe?"

"Fine," came Rachel's voice as the door to the passenger side opened and closed by itself.

Smiling a bit at her overdramatic antics, I drove to the interstate and headed home myself, hoping that I might manage to get some sleep before the sun came up.

About halfway home, an idea struck me. Jack had said that the victim was $100,000 in debt, but indebted to whom? And what did he do to get there? I tapped my phone as it hung from its holder and brought up Jack's number, pressing the call button.

"Do you know what time it is?" His irate voice spilled from the speaker of my phone.

"I'm sorry, but you said that Malcolm was in debt. Do you know who he owed the money to?"

"Can't it wait until morning?"

"One of his coworkers called me up to meet with her," I said, "and she says that he was the sort of person who never spent money. And there were these two guys who came by asking about him, saying that he owed them money."

Jack's voice changed as his interest grew. "Two guys came by?"

"I'm on my way to your place and will be there in bit."
I hung up, not waiting for an answer.

I parked in front of Jack's apartment (one of those
first floor, two-story type places) and ran to his door, not
bothering to knock as I stepped inside; he never locked
his door. "Jack?" I called as I entered his place, stepping
over a pair of shoes with dried mud on them left by the
front door.

"You shouldn't just walk inside like that," said an irritated Jack.

"Then lock your door," I replied.

He scoffed at my statement, more perturbed at me
keeping him awake all hours of the morning.

"I need your help and it's only something you can
do," I said.

"What if I don't—"

"Sit," came Tiny's voice from the far side of the living
room where a cluttered desk with a computer settled in the
middle of it.

"Tiny?" I had forgotten that he was still babysitting
Jack. "You're still—"

"Yes, he's still here," said Jack in an irritated undertone as he
walked to the chair and sat before Tiny had to ask him again.

I snatched a chair from the kitchen table, picking
up an abandoned burger wrapper and throwing it in
the garbage, and placed it next to Jack's seat. "You said
that Malcolm owed over $100,000 worth of debt, but to
whom? And how did he rack up so much? Also, did you
check his bank and credit card accounts?"

"Oh, look who's the detective?"

A growl from Tiny shut up Jack.

"No, I didn't check any of that and it's a bit illegal for me to do that."

I frowned. He was correct.

"Legality, smegality," said Tiny. "You're good at covering your tracks, right? Isn't that how you found out he owed so much money in the first place?"

Jack groaned. "I can access the police department's database remotely and see if any one there has looked into his financials."

"Do it," said Tiny, standing behind Jack with his arms crossed.

Jack didn't wait to be told twice. His hands flew over his keyboard as he typed, bringing up the police department's database and scanning the records. "Found something," he said. "It appears that new detective, Detective Henderson, has looked into the victim's finances. It's marked as for her eyes only. She's password protected everything concerning this case."

"Can you break it?" asked Tiny, never afraid to bend the law, or outright disobey it.

"I already have," said Jack. "Okay, it… this is interesting."

"What?" I asked.

"His bank accounts are untouched. He has at least eight thousand in savings and a couple in checking. No retirement accounts. If he was knee-deep in debt, you'd think he would have nothing in his accounts."

A few more minutes passed as I yawned, unable to keep my eyes open and wishing I could get some sleep.

"He has only one credit card with a balance of five hundred dollars," Jack continued.

Something didn't add up. "Could someone have stolen his identity?" I asked.

"It's possible," Jack said.

I racked my brains, trying to figure out how someone could have stolen Malcolm's identity, since he seemed to be a man who kept to himself. "You said he owed gambling debt," I said to Jack. "Is it possible that someone gambled in his name?"

"But where would we start looking?" asked Jack.

I thought back to what Keri had said about Malcolm when he had started acting strange. "Does 'double aces' mean anything?"

Jack opened a new web browser and typed in "double aces" into the search bar. One of the first results read: Double Aces' Luck of the Draw. He clicked on it and the page filled with a request for a username and password, or a link to a signup sheet. "How do we find out what he signed in under?"

"Guess that's going to take a little more digging," Jack replied.

I yawned as my exhaustion caught up with me. Knowing that Jack's attempts to learn Malcolm's sign in information would take a while, I moved to the couch, pushing the crumpled magazines to the side, and sat down. Before I knew it, my eyes closed and I fell asleep.

"Hey, get up!"

I moaned and rolled over, wishing the voice in my head, which sounded a lot like Jack's, would stop bothering me.

"Mel!"

I jerked awake, feeling groggy and rubbed the sleep from my eyes. "What?"

"I got something."

I crawled over to the computer and forced my eyes to focus on the screen.

"I couldn't figure out the victim's login information," said Jack, "but I learned which profile is his."

"How did you do that?" I asked.

"Luck, mostly," replied Jack. "Someone accidentally referred to this guy as Malcolm before apologizing for something."

I looked at the profile name that Jack pointed out to me: wildcard_2635. "That's his profile?"

"Yes. See?" He clicked on the username and it went to a profile page.

Scrolling down, I read through some of the comments and they all said the same thing: where were you, wildcard_2635? I checked the date of the earliest message and it was dated the day I had found the man in my neighbor's apartment. "So, how does this help us now?"

Jack pointed at the screen. "Because now it is active."

I looked at the last post and it read, "Been busy, but back and ready to win back my losses."

"It could just be a coincidence," I said.

"True, but there is only one-way to find out and that is to trace it."

"Huh?"

"I've developed an algorithm and as long as this guy remains online, I can trace the ISP address which might give us some leads. I already have a profile set up. We just need to be in the same game room as wildcard_2635."

Intrigued, my tiredness melted away, but there was one thing still on my mind. "I thought online gambling was illegal."

"As long as you don't gamble with real money," said Tiny, walking up behind us, placing a plate of food and a beverage in front of me. Jack started to protest but stopped upon receiving a glare from him. "Some sites let you have a certain number of tokens, free of charge, and after a certain amount of time, those tokens are refilled. You can always buy additional tokens if you choose, but that money goes to the website itself and is never doled out as winnings."

"It's similar to playing games on social media, like Farmville. You do stuff and earn coins but can always purchase more coins so that you can have the cool upgrades," said Jack. "The difference with this gambling site is that there is a secret room you can go to where you are able to use real money, but, on the surface, are the other rooms that use the tokens. To get into the secret room, you have to know someone, or prove that you are interested in upping the stakes. While you were sleeping, I did just that and received an invitation. And here is our guy right there."

Impressed, I glanced at the plate of food Tiny had given me, wondering how I was going to eat all of it as gravy dripped over the side of the dish. "What is all this?" I asked.

"The four most important food groups," replied Tiny. "Eggs, bacon, biscuits with gravy, and beer."

"I think it might be a little too early for alcohol," I said.

"Thought you might say that." Tiny took the beer, draining it in one gulp, and placed a glass of orange juice in its place. I took a sip and almost gagged from a burning sensation in the back of my throat before giving Tiny a reprimanding scowl.

"I might have added a bit of brandy to it," Tiny confessed. "It's healthy!" he said as I continued to frown at him.

I placed the orange juice to the side. Though I indulged in an occasional glass of wine or beer, I never developed much of a taste for the hard liquor, and it was still too early for such things.

"You're eating my food?" said Jack, incredulous. "And my brandy!" He turned back to the computer the moment Tiny growled at him.

"So, about this secret room," I said, hoping to distract the both of them, "our guy is here?"

"Yep," replied Jack, pointing at the avatar of wildcar_2635. "And this is us," he taps his finger next to our avatar.

Something pops up on the screen, which I assumed was the dealer typing. *Everyone ready?*

A series of yes's appeared.

I watched as cards flew across the screen toward the various players, each receiving five. "What game are we playing?"

"Poker," said Jack.

"Are you tracing him yet?" I asked.

"No," replied Jack, "he needs to say something directly to us for me to start the trace."

I frowned. This was going to take longer than I thought. I watched as players traded in cards, one by one folding, until, during the fifth game, only Jack and wildcard_2635 remained.

How many? asked the dealer.

Two, Jack typed.

He received two cards and clicked on them to see what they were: an ace of spades and a two of diamonds. Not much of a hand, considering that the other cards were a queen of hearts, a two of hearts, and a nine of clubs. A pair of twos. Not much of a hand.

"What are you doing?" I asked when Jack upped the bet.

"Goading our player," he replied.

"How do you know he won't fold?"

Tiny stepped in. "He's deep in debt, right? This is a man that doesn't back away from a bet or the chance of winning. He doesn't know when to cut his losses."

"It's a gamble," Jack added, "but one I hope pays off."

Makes sense. I watched, hoping that Jack's plan worked. It did. Wildcard_2635 increased his bet, turning the play back to Jack.

"Initiating virus," Jack whispered to himself, punching a few keys on the computer. "Now to continue the ruse."

A separate screen opened up on the monitor with lines and lines of numbers and letters, scrolling so fast that it was impossible to make out any of it.

"Not so much," Tiny stopped him when Jack upped the bet by an additional $500. "You'll scare him off. Make it seventy-five dollars."

Jack obeyed and wildcar_2635 increased his bet before calling Jack's hand. He showed his cards and the words "you lose" popped up on the screen.

Better luck next time, said wildcard_2635.

How about right now? Jack typed.

Wildcard_2635 agreed and more cards were doled out to those who remained in the game.

"Got it," said Jack.

I leaned in closer, anxious to know where this mysterious person was.

"He's local," said Jack," and at an internet café."

"What's the address?" I asked.

Jack looked it up on GPS. "That one right across the street from the local bookstore."

I grabbed my things and headed for the door.

"You're not going alone," said Tiny.

"Something tells me that I won't be alone," I called back as I walked through the door, and as though right on cue, it opened by itself before closing behind me. "Just keep me posted!" I called through the door.

I hurried to my car, typing a quick text message to Greg, asking him to meet me at the internet café, before sending one to Jackie about covering for me at work.

A new message made my phone chirp. *Handled*, replied Jackie.

I reached for the driver's door, but it refused to open. Pulling on it, a few curse words escaped my lips as my frustration intensified.

"Oh, does you mama know you talk like that?" teased Rachel, appearing behind the steering wheel.

"Will you let me in?" I asked.

"Passenger seat."

"It's my car," I said.

Rachel shrugged her shoulders. "It's either that or walking."

Annoyed, I walked to the passenger side of my own

car and got in, buckling my seatbelt. "If we get pulled over, how are you going to explain the fact that a ghost is driving my car?"

"Don't worry about it," Rachel said, passing off my concerns. "It's not like this isn't the first time."

She was correct about that. A few years ago, after we had proven my innocence when I was accused of murder, Rachel decided that Jackie and I needed a vacation, and she drove the entire way there. "Just be quick," I said to her.

"You ever see the movie *Bullet*?"

Oh, crap.

Chapter 11

I sat at a table, tapping my fingers as I watched the counters filled with people staring at their computer screens. The internet café was more of a mall-like building with tables (some with computers, some without) where people could sit and connect to the internet. A huge sign at the entrance had the local wifi's username and password. I had always assumed that most people used their cell phones to access the internet, or use them as a hotspot; but, I guess if you don't have a good plan, using the internet can eat through your data, and people do like free stuff.

In addition to having free access to computers—you just had to go to the guy at the desk to get a username and password for an individual computer—and free wifi, the café had a few restaurants inside (mostly a sandwich shop, coffee shop, or a burger place) and some stores that sold computer and phone accessories, almost a one-stop shop for those who loved their gadgets. A coffee cup slid itself into my left hand while a donut settled on my right. I stared at them for a moment, wondering why there were there, until I heard Rachel's voice.

"Eat up," she said. "You're going to need your energy. Just think. We're on a stakeout!"

A group of girls turned and glared at us with confused looks on their faces.

"Keep it down," I said.

In response, Rachel shoved the donut in my mouth, forcing me to gag as I almost choked on its coating of powdered sugar. "This is so much fun!" She shook my shoulder as I pulled the donut from my mouth. "So, how do we know which one is our guy?"

I had been wondering the same thing as I observed those typing away on their notebooks. Any one of them could be the person I searched for. I glanced at the burger place where Greg sat. He smiled, but pretended not to know me, thinking it best that we split up so that we wouldn't look conspicuous. "We need to see their screens," I said as someone strolled by with her head buried in her phone, no doubt using the free wifi so as to avoid burning through her data.

I texted Greg. *Anything?*

No, he replied.

"On it." Rachel disappeared before I could say anything. Left alone to wait for her to get back, I finished the donut and coffee, not wanting to know where she got them from, mush less how she paid for them. On a whim, I opened my wallet and chuckled when I saw a credit card in there that was not mine with a note attached to it.

Can you give this back to Tiny? I'm sure he'll want it back.

Well, it seems that she has moved on from always borrowing my money, though he didn't strike me as the type who used a credit card, but in this day and age, it is difficult to get by without one.

"Found him!" Rachel appeared beside me, yanking on my arm and hauling me from my chair as she dragged me to the computer area. I tried to act natural, but her frantic movements made such a thing difficult. The odd glances from people told me so.

"Rachel, what is it?" I asked and noticed that Greg had gotten up from his chair, worried.

"Over here!" I allowed Rachel to lead me and stopped when I saw Ian sitting at one of the public computers.

Pulling out my phone, I snapped a picture and zoomed in. The screen matched what Jack had shown me earlier.

"I told you he's guilty," said Rachel, crossing her arms in a triumphant gesture as she waited for me to agree with her.

Glancing around, I noticed Greg walking up to me and I shook my head, pointing at Ian and motioned for him to hide. He did. I ducked behind a kiosk selling protective cases for the latest smartphone just as Ian logged off the computer and stood up. I hope he hadn't see me. I watched as he left the building and headed for the parking lot. As I hurried to the exit, a voice stopped me.

"Just one moment, Miss Summers!"

Startled, I whirled around and almost gasped when I saw Detective Henderson standing behind me. What was she doing here? Greg stood some distance away and I inclined my head toward Ian, hoping that he would get the message. I needn't have worried because Rachel vanished from my side and appeared by his, startling him, before disappearing again. He ran off before the detective noticed his presence.

"Detective," I said, trying to sound innocent, but she didn't buy it.

"What are you doing here?"

"Using the internet," I replied.

Her lips formed a thin line. "And is that why you are hiding behind this kiosk?"

Busted. I started to miss running into Detective Shorts. I hoped he returned from his vacation soon. "No reason," I said.

She arched an eyebrow, telling me that she didn't believe me. Detective Henderson pulled me aside. "I know that you have little faith in the police to solve this case, but you need to let me do my job."

"But..."

"Do you think that I haven't looked into the victim's partners? Back off."

"Getting into trouble?"

I cringed. Of all the people, Jillian Mordson just had to walk up to us. Why was it she always seemed to be where I was?

"May I help you?" Detective Henderson asked, annoyed. I guessed she disliked Jillian as much as I did.

"No."

"Then, why are you butting into a private conversation?"

"I noticed Miss Summers here with you and thought that perhap—"

"You just want another story," interrupted Rachel, not caring if everyone heard her.

"Whatever business I have with Miss Summers," said Detective Henderson, "does not concern you, nor should it end up in any of your articles."

"Are you telling me what to report?" asked Jillian in a dark tone.

"I'm warning you that if you report anything you might have overheard because of your eavesdropping, that it would be impeding an ongoing investigation."

Jillian and Detective Henderson stared at one another, challenging the other's will, until Jillian backed away. "Naturally, I wouldn't want to do that. But you should know that Mellow Summers, here, has a way of being a nuisance."

Having heard enough, Rachel appeared by Jillian's side, remaining invisible to everyone but me, and whispered in her ear, "I still don't like you."

Jillian jumped, and I knew she had heard Rachel, but before she could get away, a mischievous grin crossed Rachel's face. I knew that grin. Trouble wasn't far away. A man hurried by with a tray, carrying two hamburgers, an order of fries, and two sodas just as Rachel stuck her foot out and tripped him. He stumbled forward, plowing into Jillian and the food flew from his arms, coating her. Ketchup covered the front of her KAIMILAN blouse as soda dripped from its hemline, while Jillian shot daggers at me with her eyes. I just covered my mouth with my hand, unsure of what to do as a couple of onlookers held their phones up, filming the entire spectacle.

As though forgetting herself, Rachel snatched a phone from someone and proceeded to record herself as she skipped around. "So, this is me, having some fun with a friend. Wave ;hi', Mel!"

I just stood there, frozen.

"Anyway," continued Rachel, unaware that no one could see her and only saw a phone bouncing in midair on its own, "we were having a nice relaxing night out when that woman showed up and ruined it!" She pointed at Jillian who looked as though she wanted to murder someone. Rachel stopped, glanced around, and realized that she had neglected to make herself visible. "Oops!"

She dropped the phone and it landed on the hard floor, cracking the back casing, and vanished.

"I think I should go," I said.

Detective Henderson closed her mouth, realizing for the first time that it hung open in disbelief. "That would be wise. And don't let me catch you investigating on your own again."

I hurried outside, doing my best not to lock eyes with Jillian, and ran to my car, locking myself inside.

"Well, that could have gone better," said Rachel, appearing in the passenger seat.

I gaped at her.

"Too bad we don't know where your neighbor is."

My neighbor! I had forgotten about him with everything going on. I sent Tiny a text, asking him to have Jack see if he could find a connection between him and the victim. He texted back, *Consider it done.*

A few minutes passed as I considered what my next move should be. I needed a way to search the offices where Ian, Keri, and Malcolm conducted their charitable business, but I couldn't just show up there. "I need a distraction," I said aloud.

"Zombies!" shouted Rachel.

I jerked my head up and laughed as a few high schoolers strolled past, dressed as the living dead, telling me that Halloween wasn't far away. As they laughed and talked among themselves, an idea struck me. "We need a zombie party."

"What?" Rachel leaned closer.

"I need Keri and Ian distracted so that I can look through their offices. What better way, than to have them host an event? The only problem is that these things take time. You need to plan and figure out how to get people to show up."

"Tomorrow," said Rachel.

"What?"

"The parking area across the street from their office building is public property."

"You need a permit and those things take time."

"Call Keri and tell her that you want to host a last-minute charity event or zombie walk, leave the permit to me," said Rachel.

"What about getting people to show up?" I asked.

"I know some people on the other side who are very adept at social media marketing. Trust me. They'll be people there."

"Living?"

Rachel glared at me.

"Rachel, I…" My phone was thrust into my hands already dialing Keri. Knowing that there was no changing Rachel's mind—once she decided to do something, that was it—I finished the call.

"Keri?" I said, "this is Mel. I hope I'm not calling at a bad time."

"No," said Keri, "it's okay."

"How are you doing?"

"Better. What can I do for you?"

"I know this is last minute, but I wanted to host a zombie walk charity event tomorrow, starting at eight pm, and I wanted you and Ian to help me plan it. All proceeds will go to the Dig A Well organization."

"Where were you thinking of holding it?"

"In the parking lot right across the street from your office," I replied.

"That's public property and we would have to get a permit."

I glanced at Rachel. "Something tells me you'll have no trouble getting one. I know this is last minute and if it's too much trouble…"

"No, no," said Keri, "I could use the distraction. How many people do you think will show up?"

I looked at Rachel again. "I have a feeling it will be packed."

"Well, I'll call you back in a couple hours and let you know if we got the permit. Give me your email and I will send you all the forms I need you to fill out."

I recited my email. "Thank you," I said as we hung up.

Rachel beamed, pleased with herself, but I wasn't certain if her plan would work.

"I have a class tomorrow night," I told her.

"It will be canceled," said Rachel.

"And you know this because…"

"Well, I don't think the college will allow classes to continue in a building with a few broken pipes."

Wait a minute? The Candle Shoppe suffered a broken pipe once at a very convenient time. "You didn't happen to…"

"Oh, look at the time," said Rachel, glancing at the clock on my phone. "So much to do and so little time to do it in." She disappeared, leaving me alone in my car, wondering what I had gotten myself into.

Chapter 12

I stood in the parking lot with Jackie and Greg, watching the crowd of zombie enthusiasts as they snapped selfies to post online, showcased their costumes and makeup, and talked among themselves. Mesmerized, I couldn't believe that Rachel had managed to get so many people here, but she did.

"You know," said Jackie, "when you said that you were hosting a charity event tonight where people could show up dressed as the walking dead, I never believed that so many would show up."

"Neither did I?" I mumbled. I turned to Greg. "What happened with Ian after you left the café?"

"He came here," Greg replied.

"Here?" I asked.

"Yeah, he went into his office, turned on the light, and remained there for a while."

"Do you think he used his computer for the online gambling?" Jackie asked, pushing a man dressed as the living dead, and who seemed to have had a bit too much to drink beforehand, away from her as he made snarling sounds.

"I don't know," I said. "I just know that I need to get in there. Malcolm wasn't killed in our neighbor's apartment, but he might have suffered a fatal injury before going there, and something Rachel said about him makes me want to investigate further."

"And most statistics say that you are likely to be murdered by someone you know," said Greg.

"BOO!" Rachel appeared next to us, and I jumped, releasing a frightened scream. You'd think I would be used to her comings and goings by now, but she had a way of surprising people.

Before any of us could say anything, Rachel vanished, but I had a feeling that she would turn up again.

A group of gaggling girls ran past us, wearing rags with tendrils that trailed behind them and coated in red paint to simulate blood. One had managed to do their makeup in such a way where it appeared that the side of her face had rotted away. It must have taken her hours to do and I had to give her props for her creativity. A chill breeze ruffled my shirt, causing goosebumps to form as it touched my bare skin. I scanned the crowd for Ian but found no sign of him.

"Mel?" Keri walked up to us with a tablet in her hands. "This is quite a turn out."

I smiled, not sure of what to say.

"When you called me yesterday and asked about doing this event," Keri continued, "I thought you were crazy—"

"You weren't the only one," mumbled Jackie.

"—but here are all these people, and we have raised almost two thousand dollars! Well done."

Wow! That much? I knew Rachel said she would handle it, but I never thought we would raise this much for a charity. I wondered how she had managed to do such an effective social media marketing campaign, or if she had just shown up in people's houses and threatened to haunt them until the end of eternity if they didn't show up tonight. It wouldn't be the first time she had done that.

"Thank you," I said. "Is Ian here?" I asked, hoping to glean some information about his whereabouts. "This just seems like a lot for one person to handle."

"He's over there," Keri said, pointing to a table where people signed in and left a small donation for the privilege of entering the parking lot and joining the party.

"How are you holding up?" I asked her.

Keri placed the tablet under her arm and looked around. "Honestly? It's taking everything I have to not break down. Malcolm was a good friend, but he would have wanted us to host this event because every event we hosted meant that a charitable organization received funds to help others; and I do need the distraction. Ian has been a lot of help, though. Anyway, enough of that." She wiped a few tears that had escaped her eyes. "In a few moments, we will have a zombie hunt and then you will give a short speech—no more than a minute, really—about the organization you are raising funds for."

I gulped a mouthful of saliva. It had never occurred to me that I would have to give a speech, and I was never very good at public speaking. I stole one more glance at Ian and hoped he remained distracted enough for me to sneak into the office building. "Keep a look out, will you?" I asked both Jackie and Greg and they nodded.

I meandered through the crowd of laughing and joking zombies as I wormed my way to the edge of the parking lot and toward the office building across the street, but the moment I reached the street, I was stopped.

"Well, if it isn't Mellow Summers," said a snide voice.

I spun around and found Jillian standing behind me. Where did she come from? Had she been following me again? "What are you doing here?" I asked, not even trying to be nice.

"I caught wind of this little event and imagine my surprise when I heard that you are the one who decided to host it."

"Don't you have something better to do than to always try to tarnish my reputation?"

"I think it is odd that whenever a dead body shows up, you happen to be nearby and can be found gallivanting around town in an effort to solve it. Almost like it is a form of thrill seeking for you."

"Someday," I said, "you'll have to tell me what it is I did to anger you so much."

"I don't like psychics."

I stepped closer, doing my best not to lose my temper. "I

never said I was a psychic. You did." I studied her long-sleeved, sequined dress and wondered where she had been. "Seems like so much trouble for a special trip to check up on me. Perhaps you should have stayed at your special dinner."

"Perhaps," said Jillian. "The Association of Journalism had given me an award for 2017's Best Local Journalist."

"Congratulations." I didn't bother trying to hide the sarcasm in my voice.

Jillian opened her mouth to speak but closed it the moment Keri's voice spilled over the parking area.

"Thank you all for coming," said Keri into a microphone. "In a few moments, we will have a zombie hunt, led by our group of survivors over there." She pointed to a group of people dressed like survivors of the apocalypse. "But right now, I want the lady who is hosting this event to say a few words."

Shoot! All eyes focused on me and now I needed to make a quick speech. Unable to get out of it, I strolled up to the microphone, doing my best to smile. "Thank you," I said, fumbling for words. Giving speeches is not my forte. "I am glad that you all could make it out here tonight. Um…" I turned away from the mic and whispered under my breath, "Rachel, some help please."

I guess I didn't need to ask for her assistance because at that instant the microphone was jerked out of my hands and hovered in midair.

"*Jeremiah was a bulldog!*" Rachel's voice rang throughout the parking area, wafting over the awestruck crowd.

With all eyes glued on a hovering microphone that

danced across the stage on its own, I snuck away, seizing my chance to get away from the crowd. Concealing myself in the darkness, I hurried across the street to the office building where Keri had told me she, Ian, and Malcolm conducted their charity work. The door was unlocked. Good. I opened it and went inside.

I opened the door to the first office and looked around. A picture of Keri with an older woman sitting on her desk told me all I needed to know: this was her office. I shut the door and went to the next one. It looked like it hadn't been disturbed in a few days. I rushed to the desk and opened drawers, searching through them when one revealed a phone. Odd. Most people don't leave their phones lying around, unless it was placed here because the owner assumed he would be back within a few minutes. I picked it up and pressed the power button. The screen flashed to life and I realized that the battery had ten percent power remaining. Good. Just enough for me to look at it, assuming it wasn't locked. I pressed the image of a lock on the display and swiped it across the screen. Wow. The owner didn't have it password protected.

Marveling at my luck, I looked up the phone's device information; it belonged to Malcolm. So, this must be his office, which explains the somewhat abandoned look. Neither Ian, nor Keri must have had the desire to go through his things, not that I blamed them. I opened up the contacts folder to see if he had made any recent calls, and to my surprise, my neighbor's name was listed. So, he knew him. I put the phone back in the drawer and left the office, making my way to the final one: Ian's.

I tested the door to his office and it opened, allowing me inside. Fumbling in the darkness, I found a lamp and turned it on and soft beams of light illuminated the desk with its piles of paper and a stack of folders. Wanting to be as quick as possible, I opened drawers, rifling through them, but found nothing, and flipped through the mish mesh of folders, turning up the same lack of leads. Perhaps Rachel's suspicions had been wrong. It wouldn't be the first time either of us were mistaken about a person's guilt.

I studied the computer, wondering if I should attempt to turn it on when I spotted the blue LED light telling me that the thing had been put to sleep. I flicked on the monitor and a dialog box appeared, asking for a password. Cursing and saying some words that a person probably shouldn't say, but we do it anyway, I tried typing in a few things; zombiezrule, zombiechaity, and ianisazombie_2.0.

I don't know why I typed in that last one; it's not like I had a reason to. Or did I?

Frustrated, I turned the screen back off and must have hit the power button a little too hard because the monitor scooted back a few inches, knocking something off the desk. I couldn't leave it. I scooted the monitor back in place—I didn't need anyone to know that I had been in here snooping—and hurried around the desk to grab what had fallen to the floor: a solid oak paperweight. I scooped it up and had almost put it back where it belonged when I stopped. Something sticky was on the bottom. Holding it closer to the light, I scraped at it with my fingernail, removing flecks of what appeared to be dried blood. I weighed it in my hand; the paperweight was heavy enough to be used for striking someone in the head, and Malcolm had a wound on his.

I squeezed the paperweight as I turned off the light and made my way to the door, flinging it open and stopped. Ian stood in the hallway.

"What are you doing here?" he asked.

"Nothing," I said, trying to hide my nerves as I hid the paperweight behind my back. "Just looking for a bathroom."

"That's not nothing," Ian said.

"Yes, well, I should get back."

"Bathroom is over there." Ian pointed at the restroom which was a good ten feet away from where I stood.

"Thank you." I tried to squeeze past him, but he blocked my path.

"Is there a reason why you were in my office?"

My mind raced with a multitude of excuses, but none of them sounded the least bit legitimate. "I really think I ought to get back."

Ian blocked my path again. "I'll take what's behind your back."

I gripped the paperweight tighter. "I really think..." I began.

Ian seized my arm and flung me around, snatching the paperweight from my hands when, out of nowhere, he was flung back by an unseen force. Rachel materialized between us. "I can't even leave you alone for a minute," Rachel joked to me.

Ian stared at me with a blank expression. I don't know

if he saw Rachel or not, but it was apparent that he had not expected to be thrown down the hallway. He spotted the paperweight, which had landed near the door to the restroom and leapt for it. Rachel tackled him, forcing him to the entranceway. He tried to get away, but she grabbed his shoulders and threw him out the door, dragging him across the street before chucking him into the middle of the parking lot with a bunch of stunned onlookers staring wide-eyed at the entire spectacle, unsure of what was going on. Ian tried to get away. Rachel pounced on him and penned him to the ground with his arms flailing as he screamed.

I snatched the paperweight and ran outside.

"Murderer!" Rachel yelled at him, but no one saw her. All they heard was her irate voice while they watched a man struggling against some unseen force.

"I didn't mean to!" screamed Ian.

"Yeah?" shouted Rachel, lifting Ian into the air. "Mean to do what?"

"Rachel!" I yelled, not wanting her to hurt him.

"To kill Malcolm!" screamed Ian as he hung in mid-air, unable to move.

Rachel dropped him.

"What?" said Keri, pushing her way through the crowd. "You did what?"

"It was an accident, Keri," Ian pleaded, standing up and still shaking from Rachel's manhandling of him. "I didn't mean to. It wasn't… if he would have just listened."

Keri charged Ian and sucker punched him so hard that he fell to the ground unmoving. Before she could hit him again, Greg seized her by the waist and pulled her back, whispering to her to get her to calm down just as Detective Henderson showed up with a few police officers.

"Good thing Greg called her," said Jackie, walking up behind me and referring to the detective.

"Yeah," I said as I watched the detective put Ian in handcuffs before having an officer cart him away. Still feeling the paperweight in my hands, I walked up to the detective and handed it to her. "You might want this," I said. "I think he used it to kill Malcolm."

Detective Henderson opened an evidence bag and I placed the paperweight in there, while she gave me a disapproving glare. "I told you to stay out of it."

"I thought Detective Shorts had warned you about me," I quipped, to which Detective Henderson mumbled something about being glad when he wasn't on vacation anymore.

I headed back to Jackie and Greg—he had let go of Keri so that she could give her statement to the police—and was stopped by Jillian. "What now?" I demanded of her.

"Seems that the psychic wins again. I'm going to prove you are a fraud someday."

"For the last time," I said to her, "I'm not a psychic. Get a life, bitch."

Jillian gave a sardonic grin and walked away to her car.

"Have a safe trip home," Rachel called after her, appearing by my side and waving. I watched her, not believing her innocent façade. I knew her too well.

"Safe trip?" I asked.

Rachel nodded.

"Please tell me you didn't do something to her car."

"Me?" Rachel pointed at herself. "I'm surprised at you, Mel. How could you possibly think that I would be that devious?"

"Mel!" Greg ran up to me with his phone in his hand. "I just got a text from Tiny telling me to get you over to Jack's place right away. They learned something about our neighbor."

I looked at Jackie, but she must have read my mind.

"You guys go," she said. "I'll find my own way home."

"Here," I tossed her my car keys.

Greg and I ran to his car and had to walk past Jillian's. We watched as she started her vehicle and drove away only to have all four tires pop out of their wheel hubs and roll down the street as the car skidded across the asphalt, sending sparks everywhere.

Rachel appeared behind us. "Looks like someone loosened all the lug nuts to her tires. And I did not do it." She vanished, laughing to herself and some people turned in her direction, wondering where the hysterical laughter came from.

Greg urged me to move and I followed him to his car, wondering what Tiny and Jack had discovered.

Chapter 13

The front wheel struck another pothole, jerking me to the side once again, causing me to bump into Greg who sat in the back seat of his car with me, while Tiny drove with Jack in the passenger seat. Once we had arrived at Jack's, we got a rushed story about how he had discovered where my neighbor could be and how Malcolm and my neighbor were distant cousins, which explained why he had a key to the apartment.

"You okay?" Greg asked me.

"Fine," I replied, a bit perturbed that Greg hadn't been allowed to drive his own car, but that was Tiny for you: he never let anyone drive, if he could avoid it.

Another dip in the road caused the car to jolt.

"Don't worry. I'll fix it," said Tiny.

"Who's worried?" muttered Greg.

"Heard that," said Tiny.

"I think you're going the wrong way," Jack said, holding up his phone with the GPS activated. "We should probably turn—"

"You can always walk home," growled Tiny and Jack shut up.

I wondered where Rachel was. She had disappeared after that stunt with Jillian's car. She always came and went as she pleased and there was no predicting what she would do next and—Oh my gosh! I had a project due tomorrow! I had completely forgotten about it. If we ever got home, I was going to be up all night finishing it. I was supposed to prepare a slideshow for my computer class, using multimedia in addition to text. It wasn't complicated, just time consuming.

"Turn here," said Jack.

"Which way?" asked Tiny.

"There is only one road to turn onto," snapped Jack, receiving a reproachful glare form Tiny. "Turn right," he said in a gentler tone.

Tiny steered the car onto an abandoned dirt road and inched his way down it, doing his best not to hit a tree; though some of the low-hanging branches scraped the top of the car. "I'll fix that," he said as Greg cringed from all the cosmetic damage being done to his car.

"I think there's a cabin up there," I said, trying to look through the windshield.

It turned out that my neighbor had a small cabin well outside the city, a bit of a getaway place when he needed to relax, and since cell reception was spotty out here, no one could get hold of him either. Tiny parked the car next to a vehicle that looked like it had been sitting there for a few days with gold and brown leaves coating it. I jumped out of the car and ran to the door.

"Hello! Anyone in there?" I shouted, but no one answered. The dark windows and eerie silence told me that no one was in there or had been there in a while. "No answer," I said when the others ran up to me.

"All right," said Tiny, taking charge, "we're going to split up."

"But…" began Jack, but he clamped his mouth shut when Tiny glared at him.

"You two"—Tiny pointed at Greg and me—"go in that direction. We'll go this way. If you find anything, yell."

Greg and I nodded and walked off, following a narrow path down a hill that led toward a river. I didn't know where to begin or where my neighbor was. I just hoped that he was okay before we ruined his day with the bad news about his cousin.

"Where would you go, if you were out here by yourself?" I asked Greg.

"Probably to the river to fish."

I smiled. He liked fishing, though I never cared for it, nor did I like eating fish, but he tolerated the ghosts coming and going from my life so joining him on the occasional fishing trip was the least I could do. We trekked down some makeshift stairs that appeared to be in need of repair, hoping we would find something. Focusing on the water, and my own anxiety over the possibility of finding a body, I ran, taking the steps two at a time and not paying attention to where I stepped.

"Mel!"

Greg's scream startled me, alerting me to the fact that a section of the stairs was missing, but the fallen leaves and brush concealed it. I gasped as his arm reached out and grabbed me, preventing me from falling.

"Look!" I pointed just beyond the gap and at a lump that lay further down the hill next to a tree.

"Stay here," Greg said. He moved closer to the missing steps and eased his way through it, sliding down the hill toward the lump. "Call Tiny!"

I ran up the stairs and back to the house screaming Tiny's name. He heard me and rushed to my location, demanding to know what was wrong, but all I did was point in Greg's direction. Without further explanation, Tiny and Jack hurried to the steps and spotted Greg shaking a man awake: my neighbor.

"This branch has him pinned," said Greg.

"You stay here," Tiny told me and I didn't argue. I wasn't strong enough to lift that branch.

Jack stayed with me as Tiny worked his way down the hill, underneath a section of the steps, and to Greg. They conversed among themselves for a few seconds, until Tiny stood to one side and hoisted the branch off my neighbor as though it weighed nothing. Together, they lifted my neighbor up and carried him up the hill where Jack and I waited, and we reached down to grab him. Once we had him on stable ground, Tiny and Greg hauled themselves up before leaning my neighbor over their shoulders again.

"Is he okay?" asked Jack.

"I'm fine," said my neighbor. "It's just a broken leg."

"What happened?" I asked.

"Fell through those stairs. The wood must have rotted away. When I hit the tree, it knocked an already broken branch on top of me and I was trapped."

"For how long?" I asked.

"Since, this morning," my neighbor replied. "What are you all doing here and how did you find me?"

"Property records," said Jack. "You're listed as the owner of this place."

"So why are you here? Don't get me wrong, I'm glad you are, but…"

I paused, looking at my neighbor, unsure of how to tell him the bad news. "Your cousin, Malcolm, is dead. I don't know how close you two were, but he was found in your apartment."

"What? How?"

"We'll tell you on the way to the hospital," said Greg.

We got my neighbor in the car and drove him to the nearest hospital so that he could be checked out and unloaded the details about his cousin's murder along the way. There was no good way to tell him, but he deserved to know the truth.

Chapter 14

"You ready?" I asked Keri one last time before leaving her in her office.

After we had gotten my neighbor to a hospital, I told Tiny about the two thugs who had accosted Keri, demanding that she pay back what they thought Malcolm owed, though it was really Ian's debt; he just racked it up in his friend's name. Tiny agreed to handle it. He and Sombrero waited in what was Malcolm's office, which was right across from Keri's. Jackie waited outside with Greg and her thumb rested on speed dial for the police should anything go wrong. After I had gotten home at around four in the morning, Jackie informed me that Mr. Stilton had decided to close down the store for a couple of days: something about the cash register walking out of the shop on its own only to show up at his house gift wrapped. I'll give you three guesses as to how that happened, but you'll only need one.

"Ready," replied Keri.

"Remember," I said, "Just act natural. Tiny and I are right next door."

"Okay."

I left Keri in her office and hurried into Malcolm's office where Tiny and Sombrero were.

The front door opened and two men walked inside, right on time too. Tiny had her call them and leave a message, saying that she had the money to pay them back. They strolled into her office.

"So, where's our money?" one asked.

Tiny and Sombrero stepped across the hall into Keri's office, making no noise.

"Behind you," said Keri.

The two men turned around and jumped back. Tiny's imposing presence startled everyone.

"Tiny!" one screamed and I got the feeling that just about everyone in this town knew Tiny.

"What's this I hear about you two squeezing this nice lady for some money," said Tiny, the muscles in his arms bulging.

"Us? No. We weren't—It's all a mistake!"

Tiny's eyes turned to slits. "Mistake?"

"Yeah," said one of the men.

Sombrero cracked his knuckles, causing the two men to jump.

"Nice little racket you have going on here," said Tiny. "An illegal online gambling site embedded within a legitimate one. Then, you just put the squeeze on those who owe you money. The problem is you went after a friend of mine."

"We didn't know she was a friend of yours," said one of the men.

"I suggest you leave." Tiny closed the distance between him and the men. "If I ever hear of you or anyone you know coming in here again, I'll visit you personally. You have five second to get out of my face."

Both men ran to the door and pulled on it, but it wouldn't budge.

"One!" called Tiny.

The two men struggled against the glass door, yanking on it with their combined strength, but it held firm.

"Two!"

Rachel materialized on the other side of the glass, but only I saw her. She waved and had a huge grin on her face, laughing as the frightened men tried to get out. Rachel always did like a dramatic entrance and playing pranks on people.

"Three!"

The two men beat their fists against the door, desperate to get out, but Rachel refused to budge, having the time of her life. Can you even use that word to describe a ghost? Perhaps I should use "ethereal existence", or does it really matter?

"This is so much fun!" Rachel yelled at me, laughing so hard, that if she had lungs, she would probably cough them up.

"Four!" Tiny's voice echoed throughout the building.

The two men panicked and pulled on the door one last time, the exact moment Rachel decided to let go, and they fell backward before scrambling to their feet. They bolted to their car.

I ran outside and Rachel's cackling laughter stopped me.

"I crack myself up sometimes," she said. "Oh! Almost forgot." She grabbed onto me, pressing her check against mine and snapped a picture, and don't aske me where she got the camera.

"Are you taking a selfie?" I asked.

"My fans are awaiting an update," said Rachel. "Oh! They're getting away!" Rachel vanished and I watched as the man in the driver's seat of the car was pulled to the back by an unseen force, while the other tried in vain to get out of the car but found it impossible to open the door or window. Rachel appeared behind the wheel and waved as she performed a few wheelies with the two men screaming in panic as their own car seemed to drive itself.

"This is so much fun!" yelled Rachel, having a ball.

I just watched her. There wasn't anything I could do to stop her.

"How about we go to Mexico, boys?" she shouted, copying a line from *Supertroopers*.

"How long do you think she'll keep this up?" asked Jackie.

I shrugged my shoulders. "Until she grows bored. Maybe she'll gift wrap them and dump them off at the police station."

I checked the time. "Shoot!" I said. "I have a class in twenty minutes!"

I kissed Greg and waved good-bye to Jackie as I ran

to my car and sped off to the university. I might make it there in time, but I didn't know what to do about my assignment, which never got done. Sucking it up and knowing that I will just have to take the bad grade, I hurried to the college, pulling into the parking lot and taking the first available space. I ran across campus to the building where the computer lab was kept and hurried inside, almost knocking over a couple of students as they left.

"Sorry," I called after them after receiving a few dirty glares.

I reached the door to my class and stopped. Hanging on it, in bright yellow paper, was a sign that read, "Class canceled due to a malfunction of all the computers within the lab."

"Oh, yeah, I meant to tell you," said Rachel, appearing by my side.

I jumped, having not expected her to show up like that. "You have got to stop sneaking up on me like that."

"Why?" replied Rachel. "Your facial expressions are so funny." She pretended to be scared, mocking me and I chuckled a little.

"And you wouldn't know anything about this, would you?"

"Me?" said Rachel in an innocent tone. "Not a thing. But hey! You now have a few extra days to finish that assignment."

"Saved by the ghost," I said.

"Oh! You're going to love my latest post." She grabbed my phone and looked up her fan page. I still couldn't believe she had one, much less so many followers, but this is the age of social media. "Here." She handed me back my phone.

I took it. Right there was the selfie that Rachel had taken of us as I left Keri's office with me looking startled, while Rachel had a huge smile on her face. It read:

Me and my friend Mel having just solved another mystery and helped someone being threatened
by two unsavory *bleep!*-holes. Can't wait for the
next adventure!

"Thanks, Rachel," I said.

"What are friends for? By the way, I'm going to be a bridesmaid at your wedding, right?"

Bridesmaid? I hadn't even thought that far, and how do you explain a ghost being your bridesmaid? I was planning on having Jackie as my Maid of Honor, but beyond that, I had no idea what to do. I just hoped my mother doesn't show up to plan the wedding, or worse, my Aunt Ethel.

I just smiled and nodded, saying that we should get something to eat, to which Rachel agreed.

"I know just the place," she said, leading me out the door and into the bright sunshine.

Book 15 in the series is coming soon.

About the Author

Janet McNulty currently lives in West Virginia where she continues to work on the Mellow Summers Series. She began the series two years ago as a fluke, but liked writing it so much, that she decided to stick with it.

Besides writing paranormal mysteries, Ms. McNulty has also accomplished success in other genres. She has a fantasy saga (*Legends Lost*) published under the name of Nova Rose and a new dystopian trilogy (*Dystopia*) and acience fiction series (*Solaris Saga*) as well. Ms. McNulty once referred to herself as an author who is "a little something for everyone."

She is currently busy working on the next Mellow Summers book.

Of course, writing is not the only passion in her life and every author needs some down time. When she isn't working on her books, Ms. McNulty enjoys reading and just poking around in her garden.

More by Janet McNulty

The Mellow Summers Series

Sugar And Spice And Not So Nice
Frogs, Snails, And A Lot Of Wails
An Apple A Day Keeps Murder Away
Three Little Ghosts
Oh Holy Ghost
Where Trouble Roams
Two Ghosts Haunt A Grove
Trick Or Treat Or Murder
Roses Are Red…He's Dead
Double, Double, Nothing But Trouble
Ring Around The Rosy, Not Another Ghosty
Hickory Dickory Dock The Ghost In The Clock

Violets Are Blue More Trouble Brews
Hey Diddle Diddle The Zombie In The Middle

Mellow Summers moves to Vermont to attend college, accompanied by her friend Jackie. They soon find themselves running into ghosts and one mystery after another.

The Solaris Saga

Also available in audio.

Solaris Seethes
Solaris Seeks
Solaris Strays
Solaris Soars

Every myth has a beginning.

After escaping the destruction of her home planet, Lanyr, with the help of the mysterious Solaris, Rynah must put her faith in an ancient legend. Never one to believe in stories and legends, she is forced to follow the ancient tales of her people: tales that also seem to predict her current situation.

Forced to unite with four unlikely heroes from an unknown planet (the philosopher, the warrior, the lover, the inventor) in order to save the Lanyran people, Rynah and Solaris embark on an adventure that will shatter everything Rynah once believed.

The Enchained Trilogy

Enchained
Book 2 (Coming Soon)
Book 3 (Coming Soon)

**Sworn to protect
Sworn to serve
Sworn to obey**

Having spent her entire life secluded in the Martial Training Corps, Noni passes the final test, achieving the coveted position as arbiter of Arel. Placed under the tutelage of a seasoned veteran, Noni will see her city for the first time and learn that not everything is as she had been taught to believe.

The Dystopia Trilogy

*Also available
in audio.*

Dystopia
Tempered Steel
Liberty's Torch

**Imagine living in a world where
everything you do is controlled.**

Dana Ginary lives in a world where every aspect
of her life is controlled by the Dystopian Government.
Forced to work in Waste Management, her life becomes
a nightmare with hunger and survival is her only constant. Before she knows it, she is caught up in a resistance
movement and exiled from Dystopia, forced to find her
way in the barren wastelands. While there, she must learn
to live independently and discover how far she is willing
to go to live and achieve freedom.

The Legends Lost Series

Published under Nova Rose

Tesnayr
Amborese
Galdin

Enter the Lands of Tesnayr and join on an epic fantasy adventure that spans over 1,500 years.

Begin with Tesnayr, the first king of the five lands as he unites the against a savage foe bent on their destruction.

Next, Join Amborese as she fights reclaim the throne after her family was forced to flee from it.

Thinking peace has finally entered the land, follow Galdin as he returns to Tesnayr to find it greatly hanged. Barbarians, led by a mysterious sorcerer, burn and destroy as they go. And only Galdin can stop them if he chooses to accept his fate.

Visit www.legendslosttrilogy.com to learn more about the Legends Lost Trilogy.

Grandpa's Stories

My grandfather grew up in Arizona during the 1920s and 1930s. One week after the attack on Pearl Harbor he joined the Navy. During the summer of 2012, my mother visited him and recorded his stories about growing up, World War II, and his time as an employee at the Pacific Bell Telephone Company. This is the history of the 20th century as he lived it. These recordings make up this book. These are his words.

Something for the Little Ones

The Dragon Who series

The Dragon Who was Afraid of the Dark
The Dragon Who Went to the Moon
The Dragon Who Found a Monster Party
The Dragon Who Found a Spider in His Shoe
The Dragon Who Explored the Sea
The Dragon Who Caught a Cold

The Fairy Who series

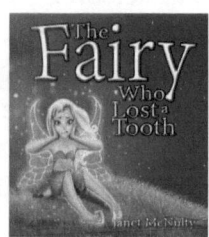

The Fairy Who Lost a Tooth
The Fairy Who Got Lost

Mr. Chili's Chili
Mr. Chili Goes To School
Mr. Chili's Halloween
Mr. Chili's Christmas

Others:

Mrs. Duck and the Dragon
The Hungry Washing Machine
Rhymes-a-lot
Are You the Monster Under My Bed?
How Do You Catch An Alien